GIRLS
TO THE
RESCUE

Tales of clever, courageous girls
from around the world

Home Safely

Edited by Bruce Lansky

Meadowbrook Press

visit us at
www.abdopublishing.com

Editor: Bruce Lansky
Coordinating Editor: Jason Sanford
Copyeditor: Christine Walske
Production Manager: Joe Gagne
Production Assistant: Danielle White
Cover Illustrator: Joy Allen

Cataloging Data

Home safely / edited by Bruce Lansky.
    p. cm. (Girls to the rescue)
    Contents: Tulia!—Dingo trouble—Railroad through and through—Gabrielle and the polar bears—Tricking the wolves—To catch a cat—Rachel's war—Anna's mystery—The clever daughter—Like father, like daughter.
    Summary: A collection of ten stories featuring admirable girls in both familiar and exotic settings.
    ISBN: 0-88166-315-8 (paperback)
    ISBN-13: 978-1-59961-132-7 (reinforced library bound edition)
    ISBN-10: 1-59961-132-5 (reinforced library bound edition)
    1. Children's stories. [1. Short stories.] I. Lansky, Bruce. II. Title. III. Series.
    PZ5 2007
    [Fic]--dc22

Contents

Tulia!

AN ORIGINAL STORY BY JOAN HARRIES

Swahili Words:

Tulia (pronounced "too-LEE-ah"): means "calm down."

Nzuri (pronounced "n'ZOO-ree"): means "good."

"Aisha, I've asked you twice already: do you want ice cream? All you do is stand there holding that glass."

"Sorry. I was thinking about something else." Aisha put the glass in the dishwasher. "Ellen, do you smell smoke?"

"Aisha, every time you go with me to baby-sit, you imagine things," Ellen said. "When I sat for the Cohens, you heard burglars. Now you smell smoke."

"I guess I do overreact. Mom says so, too."

Ellen shoved a dish of ice cream into Aisha's hand. "My favorite," said Ellen. "Ben and Jerry's Cherry Garcia. Mrs. Brownell always gets some for me when I baby-sit." Aisha and Ellen sat at the kitchen table.

"Jake liked when you helped tuck him in," said Ellen. "Did you make up that story you told him?"

Aisha nodded. "When you asked Mrs. Brownell if it was okay to bring me along, did you tell her I'm African American and . . . "

"No. Why should I?"

"Just wondered. Lots of people in Vermont act surprised when they meet me. I guess there aren't many African Americans here, 'specially—Ellen! I'm not imagining this time. Something's burning!"

"So why didn't the detectors go off?"

Aisha's spoon clattered in her dish as she jumped up. "My nose works better than a smoke detector. And it doesn't need batteries . . . which people forget to replace sometimes." She walked over to the stove. "Maybe Mrs. Brownell forgot to turn the oven off, and some spills are burning."

"Maybe. She's always in a hurry," said Ellen.

Aisha opened the oven door. "No, it's cold."

"Nothing burning in the microwave or toaster either. I'd better check on Jake." Ellen dashed out.

Smoke stung Aisha's eyes as she followed Ellen through the living room.

"The lights went out!" Ellen's voice shook. "Aisha, I'm scared."

"Who isn't?" Aisha grabbed Ellen's arm. "Jake! Come on!"

"*Tulia,*" Aisha told herself. Aisha's mom often said that to her. *Tulia* is a Swahili word. It means calm down. Aisha's mother learned it when she studied African languages. "*Tulia,*" Aisha kept reminding herself as she headed for the stairs.

"Don't go up!" cried Ellen. "Remember when the firefighter came to our school? She said, 'Leave the building immediately, then call the fire department.'"

"And leave a . . ." Aisha was going to say, "And leave a two-year-old to burn to death?" But there was no sense in talking now.

She ran up two steps. On the third, a blast of smoke overcame her. She slumped against the wall, gasping for breath.

"Come with me!" yelled Ellen. "I'm going out to call 911."

Smoke enveloped Aisha. What if she died of smoke inhalation? When Mrs. Brownell came home, she'd find Aisha's body on the steps and little Jake. . . .

"*Tulia!*" Aisha told herself. She remembered the firefighter's words: "Crawl. The best air is near the floor."

Aisha sank facedown on the steps. Mouthfuls and nosefuls of dust weren't so great, but they sure were better than suffocating. Coughing and sneezing, Aisha dragged herself up two more steps.

The firefighter had said: "Cover your nose and mouth with a damp cloth."

A towel. The bathroom was at the top of the stairs.

Step eleven. Aisha heard sounds like logs crackling in a fireplace. She couldn't tell what part of the house was burning. What if Jake's room was on fire? She knew smoke could kill. And there was no sound from Jake!

"Don't get hysterical," Aisha warned herself. "Little kids can sleep through anything."

Step thirteen. She reached for the next step, but there was none. Just flat, lovely floor.

Aisha felt around. The bathroom door was open. She crawled in, felt the smooth, cool tub, and grabbed towels from the rack. She dumped them in the tub and turned the water on.

Wringing the heavy towels was a struggle. They were still dripping as she put one to her hot face. Aisha could almost hear the sizzle.

She draped another towel over her head and sucked in breaths of damp, filtered air. She held the third towel under her arm and crawled to Jake's room.

"Jake," Aisha called, forcing herself not to scream. If he panicked, she'd never be able to get him out.

After bumping into a table and who-knows-what-else, Aisha found the bed. "Jake." Kneeling, she leaned over him. She heard soft baby breaths. "Thank you, God," she whispered.

Bedsprings squeaked as Jake stirred and sat up. "I want my mommy!"

Aisha's instincts told her: grab him and run down the stairs. But dealing with Jomo, her little brother, had taught her she was no match for a kicking, punching two-year-old.

"I want my mommy," Jake whimpered.

Will he ever see her again? Will I ever see my mom? "Stop it," Aisha told herself.

"Jake, your mommy's coming soon. I'm Aisha. Remember? I told you the story about Lu, the lonely pig. And you kissed me good night."

"Aisha." Jake poked her towel. "Wet."

"I'm playing firefighter. That's why I'm wearing a wet towel. Firefighters cover their mouths and noses to keep smoke out. Do you want to play firefighter?"

Before Jake had a chance to say no, Aisha wrapped the towel around his head.

"I'm covering your face. You'll be a firefighter like me."

"Aisha and Jake firefighters."

"I'm going to pick you up and carry you outside. Put your arms around my neck and hold on tight."

Jake pushed her aside. "Pooh! Jake save Pooh."

"Dear God," thought Aisha. "Will we ever get out of here?" She grabbed Jake's arm.

"Ow!"

Tulia! "Sorry, Jake, I didn't mean to hurt you, but firefighters have to work fast."

By this time Jake had found Pooh. He took Aisha's hand. "Me go fast."

"I'll zip Pooh up inside your pajamas," Aisha told Jake, "so he'll be safe."

With Pooh inside his sleeper, Jake clutched Aisha's neck. Aisha held him with one arm and crawled toward the stairs.

Pain jabbed Aisha's neck as she sat down onto the top step. "Noise!" Jake yelled. His fingers dug into Aisha's neck.

"Yes, Jake, sirens. Fire trucks are coming. Jake, we're going to slide down step by step. You're doing great. Hang on."

They bumped down one more step. Ten to go.

On the fourth step, gravity took over. Aisha gasped as they tumbled down. Jake hollered. The towels fell from their heads.

They landed in a heap in the front hall. Aisha picked up Jake and stumbled out the front door. "Jake, we made it! Are you okay?"

"Jake okay," he whispered. Aisha figured he didn't have enough breath to speak louder. He'd inhaled a lot of smoke.

"Take deep breaths, Jake. Like this." As long as she lived, Aisha knew she'd never forget the taste, smell, and feel of those first gulps of fresh air.

Behind her, she heard vicious snapping and crackling. Her whole body ached, but she had to get Jake and herself away from the burning house.

Even when Aisha finally thought it was safe to put Jake down on the grass, she still held on to him.

She laid her head against Jake's. No need to say *tulia* anymore. Everything was *nzuri, nzuri, nzuri*—good, good, good.

Suddenly Aisha heard, "Hey, guys! It's the girl and the little kid."

"Firefighter!" murmured Jake.

Big, strong hands took him from Aisha.

"What's this in your pajamas, kiddo? Oh, I see. Here, hold Pooh. He's glad to be out."

"Jake save Pooh."

"You sure did, Jake," said the firefighter. "Now I'll take you to your mother. There she is, behind the fire emergency line. Will she ever be proud of you!"

Aisha heard Ellen call out, "Aisha, thank God you're all right!" Then she heard the firefighter say, "And you, young lady, are a hero! Follow me, okay?"

"Sir," said Aisha, "do you mind if I hold on to you?"

"You're going to pass out or something? Want one of the guys to carry you?"

"No, sir. I'm blind."

The firefighter was silent for a second. "Blind! Well, I'll be darned!"

Dingo Trouble

AN ORIGINAL STORY BY DEBRA TRACY

Australian Words:

Dingo: a wild dog native to Australia.

Station: means "ranch."

Too right: means "you bet."

Mum: means "mom, mother."

Good on ya: means "good for you."

After breakfast, Samantha and Stephanie sat at their kitchen table, listening intently to their dad. "The police think a pack of dingoes killed our calves," he said. "We lost five of them today." He looked very serious. "Be careful when you're playing, girls. If dingoes are roaming the area, I want you to stay inside. And, to keep you safe, I'll leave Beau behind to protect you."

The twins cheered at this—even two-year-old Mikey happily banged his spoon on the table. Beau was the children's favorite cattle dog. He was playful and gentle, with a handsome white face and a roguish blue patch around his right eye. He helped round up the cattle on the family's station, which sprawled west of the Great Dividing Range in Australia. Because Beau was a work dog and not a pet, the twins didn't get to play with him too much.

After their dad left, Samantha and Stephanie talked about the wild dogs as they washed the dishes.

"Makes you want to stay inside, doesn't it?" Stephanie said, plopping the dirty dishes into the soapsuds. Foamy bubbles splashed everywhere.

"Too right!" Samantha replied. "But we can't stay in all summer. I'd go crazy!"

"Maybe Dad will teach us to use a rifle, now that we're twelve. Wish we knew how already. Samantha! You're not rinsing all the soap off!"

"Sorry, Stephanie. I was thinking about those dingoes. We'll have to be careful when we go outside." Samantha sighed. Both twins knew that with their mum off visiting her parents, and their dad working, it was up to them to take care of Mikey.

The rest of that morning, Samantha and Stephanie kept Mikey inside the house. They all had fun brushing and playing with Beau. By late afternoon, though, they were bored and decided to risk going outside. First, they scanned the dusty, barren horizon by peering out every window of their ranch-style house.

"I don't see any dingoes," Samantha said. Stephanie agreed. They burst outdoors and spent the rest of the day running with Beau and playing with Mikey on their back yard swing set.

The week passed uneventfully and Samantha and Stephanie forgot all about the wild dingoes.

On the day Mum was due home, Samantha and Stephanie got up early and cleaned the house. Their father smiled when he saw them hard at work. "Your mum's going to be proud of how responsible you two have been with her gone," he said, opening the freezer and taking out some wrapped steaks. "We'll cook these tonight to celebrate her coming home."

Stephanie and Samantha waved good-bye as their dad drove off. When they were finished cleaning, the house looked so good they decided to stay outside so they wouldn't mess anything up. They took Mikey and Beau and headed for the swing set, as usual. Stephanie helped Mikey climb up the metal ladder to the platform attached to the slide. After playing for a while under the hot sun, Samantha jumped off her swing. "I'm thirsty!" she said. "I'll get us some orange juice."

"Juicy! Juicy!" Mikey called. "Wheeee!" he squealed, zooming down the slide.

Beau bounded playfully after Samantha and trailed her into the house. Samantha was opening the refrigerator when she heard Stephanie screaming and Mikey wailing. Growling, Beau raced to the window and jumped onto the kitchen table to see out. He tore at the screen with his claws, and would have jumped right through it if Samantha hadn't grabbed his neck.

What Samantha saw outside made her heart jump into her throat. Stephanie was standing on the metal slide platform, clutching Mikey to her while three snarling dingoes circled them.

When the dingoes heard Beau barking, they ran to the window and leaped at him, their big paws scratching at the screen. Samantha slammed the window shut. She stood frozen with fear.

"Samantha, help!" Stephanie shrieked.

Samantha didn't know what to do. "Beau, come!" she commanded, pulling him off the table. Beau ran to the back door and clawed at the wood, desperate to get outside. If he had his way and got outside, the dingoes would tear him to pieces. Beau was a strong, loyal dog who would fight to the death to protect his people. But he was no match for three bloodthirsty dingoes.

"I'm sorry, boy!" Samantha said. She ran to the mobile radio in her parents' bedroom.

"Base to mobile one! Come in, Dad! Dad, this is Samantha. Can you hear me?"

"This is Dad," a reassuring voice replied. "What's wrong, Samantha?"

"It's the dingoes, Dad! They've got Stephanie and Mikey trapped on the swing set!"

"I'll be there as soon as I can. But it'll take me thirty-five minutes or so. I'll call the police. You stay inside!" The radio went dead. Dad was on the way.

Samantha ran back to the window. Stephanie was shuffling around on the platform to avoid the dingoes' snapping jaws. She could only imagine how her sister must feel, watching the dingoes' pointed ears, sharp eyes, and bared teeth bobbing in and out of view. The platform on which Mikey and Stephanie were perched was their only hope for safety.

"Hang in there, Stephanie! Dad's on his way!" Samantha yelled, opening the window slightly.

Suddenly, one of the dingoes made a run for the ladder, climbing halfway up before falling backwards to the ground. Stephanie screamed. A second dingo rushed the first and they fought viciously in the dirt. Soon the second dingo backed off. The first one had torn ears and a tawny, shorthaired coat tattooed with battle scars. It was obviously the leader.

The dingoes surrounded Stephanie, jumping at her from three sides, gnashing their yellow teeth. Stephanie had to stand exactly in the middle of the platform to avoid their snapping jaws. Mikey cried in her arms.

"You're doing great, Stephanie," Samantha yelled.

Stephanie didn't answer, but the dingoes ran toward Samantha's voice. They paced back and forth under the window, then bounded back to the swing set. Samantha noticed Stephanie's knees buckling a bit.

Samantha thought frantically. How could she help? She thought about sending Beau outside. He would be killed, but maybe, during the diversion, Stephanie and Mikey could get inside the house.

Beau whined and barked at the door. Samantha couldn't bear to think of losing him. She would let him out only as a last resort.

The dingoes were fighting again. Samantha watched as Stephanie leaned out towards the swings. Was she losing her ballance? She might fall!

"Stephanie! Just stay where you are! Dad's coming!"

But Stephanie seemed determined. With Mikey on her right hip, she leaned over and grabbed the chains of Mikey's baby swing. Stephanie pushed the swing so hard, it looped over the top of the swing set. The swing now dangled further from the ground.

Stephanie sent the swing flying around again and again. Each time the swing wound around the top of the swing set, it rose higher and higher off the ground. Finally, Stephanie looked satisfied. She kissed Mikey's cheek, then took off her sneaker and flung it as far as she could. As the dingoes bolted after the shoe, Stephanie leaned far over the swing set and plopped Mikey into his swing. Stephanie pulled the safety harness down and snapped him securely into his seat. Mikey's legs dangled from the swing, but he was so high off the ground, the dingoes would never reach him.

"Good on ya, Stephanie!" Samantha yelled.

Stephanie's trick infuriated the dingoes. The lead dingo leaped at the ladder again and almost climbed up. Stephanie kicked the dingo, and it fell backward, foam spraying from its mouth.

As Samantha watched, Stephanie swayed slightly. It wasn't even noon yet, but the sun was beating down and the metal swing set was getting hot.

Samantha realized she had to do something. She ran from window to window, scanning the horizon. "Hurry, Dad! Hurry!" But he wasn't in sight. With tears pouring down her cheeks, Samantha walked toward the back door. "I'm sorry, boy. I don't want to do this, but you're our only hope…" She turned the doorknob to let Beau out. Then she suddenly remembered the steaks Dad was going to barbecue for dinner. A plan formed in her head as she let go of the knob. Beau barked a sharp rebuke. "You'll thank me for this later," Samantha said. "*If* my plan works."

Samantha grabbed a butcher knife and hacked the steak into large chunks. It grew quiet outside and she anxiously peeked out the window. The dingoes were sitting on their haunches, panting. Maybe they were tired out. Maybe they'd just sit there until help came, and Samantha wouldn't have to carry out her plan.

Suddenly, the lead dingo began howling and the other two joined in. They stood up and started circling the swing set again. Stephanie stood calmly in the middle of the platform, staring. Samantha didn't like the way her sister looked. She'd rather Stephanie were crying or screaming—anything but standing dazed like that.

Samantha quickly scooped the steak chunks into a bowl. Taking a deep breath, she walked through the side door that lead to the garage. "Sorry Beau," she said, shutting the door before he could follow her. Through the garage window, Samantha could see the dingoes, tongues and drool hanging from their mouths. The back door to the house was twenty feet to her right; the swing set about sixty feet straight ahead. She hoped she could reach the door quickly enough. Samantha tried to swallow, but her mouth was so dry that her tongue stuck to the roof of it.

"Here goes…" Samantha murmured.

Samantha dropped a pile of meat onto the cement floor, then opened the back door to the garage. The dingoes were focused on Stephanie and Mikey and didn't see her. She tiptoed across the scrubby grass, dropping chunks of meat the entire way. She was ten feet from the back door to the house when the dingoes saw her.

"Samantha!" Stephanie screamed. "Get inside!"

Samantha ran. She barely felt the ground under her feet as she grabbed the door knob. Samantha heard the dingoes growling a few feet behind her. She jumped inside, slamming the door shut.

Samantha sat down on the kitchen floor with a thud. Beau licked her face and whined with worry.

"I'm okay," she said, hugging Beau. Samantha stood up and walked to the window. The dingoes were eating the meat. She watched as first the pack leader, then the other two dingoes, followed the steak trail into the garage.

Once all three dingoes were in the garage, Samantha cracked open the back door and sneaked across the grass. When she heard the dingoes chomping on the meat, Samantha ran to the garage door. Slam! She shut the door so hard the whole wall shook.

"I did it!" she yelled. "I shut the dingoes in the garage!" Samantha ran to the slide. "They can't hurt us now, Stephanie!"

Stephanie's legs gave out and the twins sat on the platform together, crying and holding each other. Mikey smiled from the swing.

"What were you thinking all that time?" Samantha asked.

"I don't know," Stephanie said weakly. "Mostly about Mikey, and keeping him safe. Sometimes I couldn't think at all—I was that scared! I also thought about how we were responsible for Mikey. I just knew that I had to save Mikey, so he'd be safe if…if…you know."

Samantha did know, and the girls grew quiet. A few minutes later a police truck pulled up. Right behind it, Dad came roaring up the driveway in his Jeep. Spotting his kids on the swing set, he drove straight to them across the grass.

"The dingoes are trapped in the garage!" Samantha cried. The police ran to the garage.

"Are you okay?" Dad asked.

"Yes," Samantha replied.

They heard three gunshots. The twins looked at each other with relieved smiles on their faces. The dingoes would never bother them again.

Later that evening, after the twins and Mikey had bathed and gotten some rest, Mum's dusty Land Rover pulled into the drive.

"Mum's home!" Samantha and Stephanie shouted excitedly.

Mum burst in the door, and threw her arms around her family. "I missed you!" she said. "Was it too boring with me gone?"

Mum didn't know what to think when her husband, the twins, and even Mikey—who always giggled when someone else did—burst out laughing.

"What? What did I miss?" Mum asked. "And why is everyone dressed up?"

"Samantha and Stephanie are going to receive medals for their bravery tonight," Dad announced proudly. "And you're just in time. We're expecting our ride soon."

"Medals? Bravery?" Mum exclaimed.

But Mum's words were drowned out by the sound of a police helicopter landing in the front yard. She looked at the helicopter, then back at Dad with a perplexed smile. "Okay, what's going on?" she asked.

"Samantha and Stephanie are heroes, that's all," Dad answered. "The police and some of the other stations want to honor them. So we're going to town. Come on girls, everyone. You, too, Beau."

"Beau?"

Samantha and Stephanie laughed, and—each taking an arm—led Mum out to the helicopter. "We've had quite a day, Mum! We'll explain it all to you on the way."

Railroad Through and Through

An Original Story by Cynthia Mercati
(Based on a True Story)

Kate Shelley loved the railroad more than anything. She loved the thrill of adventure she felt at the very sight of the burly trains. She loved listening to them roar past her family's Iowa farmhouse, some heading east toward Chicago, some bound west, toward the big Des Moines River Bridge and beyond. She loved wondering about the passengers and imagining their destinations.

Once, the railroad had sustained the Shelley family. Kate's father had worked on the Chicago and Northwestern Railway. Every morning he'd headed off to work, whistling happily but off-key, his sinewy muscles dancing under his flannel shirt. He'd loved his job as a section foreman, and like Kate, he'd loved the trains that zipped across Iowa's prairies.

But her father was gone now. Three years earlier, he'd been killed in a railroad accident.

"Your father died as he would have wanted: working on the rails," Mrs. Shelley had told her children.

Now the family depended on their tiny farm, which was no more than a patch of pasture tucked in the rolling bluffs between the Des Moines River and Honey Creek. As the oldest child, fifteen-year-old Kate had many responsibilities. She was in charge of the vegetable garden, she helped with the plowing and planting, she gathered firewood, and she cared for her younger siblings. The whole family worked long, hard hours. But at the end of every month, they still struggled to pay the bank what they owed on the farm.

Still, they managed to get by. At night, as Mrs. Shelley mended clothes and the children sat in front of the fire, they often talked wistfully about the happy times that had gone before, when their father was alive.

But on this night, July 6, 1881, the younger children were asleep, and Mrs. Shelley was sewing. Kate sat by the window, watching as lightning lit up the sky and rain fell in heavy sheets.

Suddenly, Kate called out. "Ma, look!" As Mrs. Shelley rushed to her daughter's side, Kate pointed out the window. "Honey Creek's over its banks. It's rising faster than I've ever seen!"

Mrs. Shelley laid a reassuring hand on Kate's shoulder. "Don't worry. We've been through storms before."

Mrs. Shelley returned to her sewing, but Kate was fixed at the window. The Shelleys' little farmhouse nestled right beside a small bluff that led up to the Honey Creek railroad bridge. Many times Kate had clambered up that bluff to look down at the usually friendly water. Tonight, Honey Creek looked like a witch's cauldron, bubbling and boiling.

"We have been through storms before," Kate thought, "but we've never been through one like this!"

The driving wind squealed through the loose chinks in the cabin wall, and the rain continued falling in torrents. Suddenly, the shrill whistle of a train pierced through the thunder.

"Sounds like a pusher engine," Kate told her mother. "I recognize its whistle." A pusher engine was one of the locomotives that sat by the side of the tracks until they were needed to help push or pull trains up a slope.

"Railroad men!" Mrs. Shelley said with fond exasperation. "Who else would be out on a night like this!" She shook her head and looked at Kate. Each knew the other was thinking of Kate's father. "I'm railroad through and through!" he'd loved to boast. "If I have to get a train somewhere, nothing can stop me!"

The engine's bell clanged twice—and then a new noise crashed through the night. It was the sound of shattering timbers, followed by men screaming.

"The bridge!" Mrs. Shelley exclaimed. "The Honey Creek Bridge must have collapsed!"

Without a word, Kate dashed for the door. She yanked on her heavy boots and grabbed her coat from its peg. Her mother was right behind her, pulling her back. "Where do you think you're going?"

Kate jerked on her scarf and tied it under her chin. "To help those men!"

"Kate, you can't go out in this!" Mrs. Shelley gestured helplessly toward the door. "If only your pa were here—he'd know what to do!"

"If Pa were here, he'd be out that door in a flash!"

Mrs. Shelley shook her head. "Kate, there's a big difference between what a man can do and what a fifteen-year-old girl can do!"

Kate's head went up, and her chin—clefted and strong, just like her father's chin—was set stubbornly. "Pa was railroad through and through—and so am I!" Her eyes flashed. "I've got to do what I can!"

Mrs. Shelley looked at Kate for a moment, then reached for the small lantern that hung by the door. She handed it to her daughter. Tenderly, she pulled the collar of Kate's coat close around her throat.

"Be careful," she said softly, "and come home safe. I couldn't bear to lose you, too."

"Don't worry, Ma," Kate said, then she headed outside. The wind and rain pummeled her like a prizefighter. Gasping for breath, she fell back against the door. "Maybe Ma was right," she thought. "Maybe this isn't a night for a girl to be out!" But she gathered her courage, held her lantern high, and struck out.

She waded through the flooded front yard and turned onto the path that led up the bluff. Kate had to fight the wind and rain to keep her balance. She was out of breath when she reached the crest of the hill.

Just a few minutes ago, a sturdy wooden trestle had spanned the creek. Now all that remained of the Honey Creek Bridge were some ragged timbers. A small section of the pusher engine jutted out of the water. Frantically, Kate waved her lantern back and forth, trying to signal the men whose cries she'd heard earlier. Almost immediately a gust of wind blew out the puny light. But the men had already seen it.

"Hullo!" they shouted.

Kate set down her now-useless lantern and cupped her hands around her mouth. "How can I help you?"

"We're all right!" one of the men shouted back at her. "It's the people on the Midnight Express you've got to help!" He paused to draw a breath. "I'm the engineer and this is my brakeman. We had orders to take the engine out and look for trouble—and we sure found it! The Midnight Express will be headin' right this way, and it won't know anything 'bout the bridge collapsin'!" He coughed from the strain of shouting over the storm. "It'll smack into the water—with hundreds of people on board!"

"Don't worry!" Kate shouted back. "I'll get word to it!" Then, suddenly, she wondered—how was she going to do that on a night like tonight?

Maybe she could go home, relight her lantern, climb back up the hill, and flag down the train as it approached. No, that was no good. Even if the lantern didn't blow out again, the engineer would never spot its feeble light in this storm. There had to be another way.

Kate stood stock-still, mentally scanning all the things her father had told her about how the railroad worked. "How were the stations alerted to impending danger?" she wondered. "Of course! By telegraph!"

Moingona was the nearest railroad station. If she could make it there, she could tell the telegraph operator about the collapse of the bridge, and he could send her message crackling eastward through the wires. The Midnight Express could be stopped at one of the stations before Honey Creek. She had to get to Moingona as quickly as possible.

If she hitched up the horse and rode to the station, she'd have to take the road that wound through the bluffs, and that would take far too long. Even now the Midnight Express might be starting out. The only other way to reach Moingona Station would be to follow the tracks to the big Des Moines River railroad bridge, and then cross the bridge. The station was on the other side.

The Des Moines River Bridge was a ladder of wooden crossties about two feet apart stretching nearly seven hundred feet across the water. It was hard to walk the bridge even in good weather, and people seldom attempted it. To try crossing it tonight, in the midst of this terrible storm, would be very dangerous. A shiver of fear shot down Kate's spine. Could she do it?

Kate drew a deep breath. It wasn't a question of whether she could do it—she *had* to do it. "Hundreds of people," she thought, "and I'm the only one who can save them."

Kate turned and started along the tracks, head down against the wind and pelting rain. When she reached the slope that led to the Des Moines River Bridge, she stood for a moment, staring up. Only now did she realize how much steeper it was than the little hill she'd climbed to reach the Honey Creek Bridge. She mustered all her determination, then bent almost double and half-crawling, Kate fought her way up. Finally, she reached the top— and the big bridge.

Panting, Kate peered through the rain, straining to see the other bank. But she couldn't. The bridge seemed to stretch away until it was swallowed up in blackness. If she tried to cross, would she, too, be swallowed up?

Kate tossed her head, trying to shake away her fear. "You're just dawdling, Kate Shelley," she chided herself. "Now get going!"

By now the storm was so fierce, she could barely stand up. How could she keep her balance stepping from wooden tie to wooden tie? She couldn't. "I'll have to crawl," she whispered to herself. "It's the only way."

Kate dropped to her knees. Normally, the bridge rose high above the river, but now the angry water seemed to be churning just below her. One wrong move, one slight slip, would plunge her down into it. With the wind and rain tearing at her, Kate started inching forward.

With only lightning flashes to show the way, Kate relied on touch to guide her. She would reach out one hand to find the next tie, then crawl over it. Reach out, crawl over. Inch by dogged inch, Kate made her way forward. Reach out, crawl over. Again and again. Kate cut her hands and legs on the twisted spikes and nails that studded the ties; her face was numb with cold. But she kept going. The river raged below her, splattering her with foam.

KENNEDY

Reach out, crawl over. How far had she come? How much farther did she have to go? She had no way of knowing. She only knew that she had to keep going. Reach out, crawl over. Reach out—nothing there!

One of the ties was missing.

Screaming, Kate fell forward. Her right hand shot out, and she grabbed the iron rail. She was dangling over the river now, feet flailing the air. Gasping and half crying, she pulled her other arm up to grip the rail with both hands. The wind yanked the scarf off her head. She saw it swirl helplessly in the wind, then disappear. Would she, too, disappear into the storm?

Kate tightened her grip, wincing with the effort. With more strength than she'd known she possessed, she pulled herself up until she was again kneeling on one of the wooden crossties.

Breathing in violent jerks, Kate huddled on the bridge. Her heart was beating so hard, she could hear it. She was dizzy; her stomach was churning. She had almost fallen. If she went on, she would surely fall!

How would it feel to plunge into that rushing river? How long would it take for the current to squeeze the breath out of her lungs? Kate willed her heart to slow. She swallowed, took a deep breath, then took another. She knew she had to fight down her panic, or she'd be lost—and with her, the only hope of hundreds of people.

"I can do it," she muttered in jerky bursts. "I can!"

Kate gritted her teeth. Tie by tie she was going to conquer this bridge! She had to. Reach out, crawl over. Her muscles were cramped and aching, and her eyes stung with tears against the cold. When she finally reached the end of the bridge and stood, her legs trembled, exhausted. But she couldn't afford to rest. Moingona Station was still a half-mile away. Kate started running down the tracks, slipping on the wet ties again and again, then struggling to her feet. But she didn't stop; she couldn't. Finally, she saw the faint lights of the railway station beckoning her.

The telegraph operator and several other railroad men were seated inside the station around a pot-bellied stove, hands outstretched. As Kate crashed into the room, their heads jerked around. Her red hair was plastered to her head, and she was gasping for air.

"The Honey Creek bridge!" Kate rasped at the started men. "It's collapsed!

The operator jumped to his feet. "Are you sure about that?"

Kate nodded. "I'm Kate Shelley; our farmhouse is right next to the bridge! You've got to warn the Midnight Express!"

Without another word, the telegraph operator ran to his desk. Kate sagged onto one of the wooden benches that ringed the room. She was dazed with exhaustion; still, she smiled as she heard the urgent tapping of her message across the telegraph wires.

But had her warning come in time?

The other men gathered around the telegraph desk, waiting for the reply. Kate stayed on the bench. The only sounds to be heard in the room were the hissing stove, the roaring storm, Kate's ragged breathing, and the ticking of the clock.

Then they heard a reply being tapped back. Quickly, the operator translated. "The Midnight Express has been warned and halted. Everyone's safe!"

The men cheered, but Kate Shelley was not finished yet. She forced herself to stand on her wobbly legs. "The pusher engine—the engineer and his brakeman—they're stranded in Honey Creek!"

"We'll send out a rescue party," the operator said. He surveyed the bedraggled girl. "But you'd better stay put. You've done enough for one night."

Kate wouldn't be put off. "Your party would have trouble finding them in the dark. I know exactly where they are. I promised myself I'd help those men, and I'm not going to quit now!"

Quickly, the railroad men climbed aboard an engine sidetracked in the Moingona Station yard. Several of the men rode atop the engine. Kate, wrapped in a blanket, sat in the cab. The engine pulled away from the station and headed onto the Des Moines River Bridge.

The engine stopped well before Honey Creek. Quickly, Kate led the railroad men to the crest of the bluff, where they could see the engineer and brakeman in the water, still clinging to the wrecked pusher engine. As she watched, thick ropes were lowered into the water and the stranded men grabbed on gratefully. Slowly, they were hauled out of the creek. Only when Kate saw that the two men were safe on the bank did she allow one of the rescuers to lead her down the hill and home.

Alerted by the noise of the rescue, Mrs. Shelley was standing at the door of the farmhouse. When she saw a lantern swinging through the darkness, Mrs. Shelley ran down the path and gathered her daughter in her arms. "Kate," she breathed, "tell me that you're all right!"

Bone-weary and shivering uncontrollably, Kate smiled. "I'm fine, Ma," she said, "only a little cold."

Mrs. Shelley led Kate into the cabin, and the railroad man followed them. "You don't know how worried I was, Kate," her mother murmured. Now Margaret, Mayme, and John came running into the kitchen. They mobbed Kate, tugging at her coat and demanding answers, all of them talking at once.

"She's a brave girl, your daughter," the railroad man told Mrs. Shelley above the babble. "I still can't quite believe what she did tonight!"

"I can!" Mrs. Shelley said quickly. Her eyes sparkled with tears of relief, and one arm was wrapped firmly around Kate. "Kate is railroad through and through!" Mrs. Shelley said. She pressed her lips against Kate's wet hair, whispered, "You did all of us proud tonight, Kate—but especially your pa. You did just what he would have done! Tonight there was another Shelley working on the rails."

In recognition of Kate's heroism, *The Chicago Tribune* paid off the mortgage on the Shelley farm. In addition, a bridge across the Des Moines River was named in her honor. It's called the Kate Shelley High Bridge, and it crosses the river not far from the site of Kate's big adventure.

Gabrielle and the Polar Bears

AN ORIGINAL STORY BY DEBRA TRACY
(BASED ON A TRUE STORY)

French Words:

Pourquoi (pronounced "por-KWA"): means "why."

S'il vous plait (pronounced "seel voo play"): means "please."

It was a frosty December morning, but Gabrielle didn't even notice the cold. She had to be the luckiest girl ever. Her older sister, Nicole, worked as a zookeeper near their home in Lyons, France, and she'd given Gabrielle permission to help her after school and on weekends. Gabrielle was only twelve, but she already knew she wanted to be a veterinarian.

Gabrielle watched while Nicole locked Josephine and Napoleon, two adult polar bears, out of their cage's holding area so she and Gabrielle could clean it. The electric door slid shut with a clang. The bears knew the routine: when the door reopened, a delicious breakfast would await them. They snorted impatiently and pawed at the heavy metal door.

"I think of the bears' holding area as their own cozy house," Gabrielle said. "The door we just locked is their front door. They wait out in the front yard while we clean their house and make their meals. When you think about this way, we're the polar bears' maids."

Nicole laughed and unlocked the zookeeper's door with a key attached to her belt. "Maybe someday I'll have my own key, too," Gabrielle thought. She grabbed a broom and a bucket of disinfectant and stepped through the narrow door into the bear's "house."

Gabrielle and Nicole cleaned the holding area, then piled fresh hay in one corner. When they were finished, Nicole and Gabrielle walked back outside and pulled the zookeeper's door shut. They carefully weighed the bears' vegetables, herring, and dry kibble and poured the food through chutes in the wall. Gabrielle then lifted the lever that slid open the "front door," allowing the bears back into the holding area. The two huge creatures ambled toward their food.

"Did you see Josephine?" Gabrielle asked Nicole as they returned to the feed room. "Her belly is almost dragging on the ground!"

"Josephine will deliver her cub any day now," Nicole said while Gabrielle crumbled moist cat food into a bucket. "I'm going stay here at night just in case Josephine delivers her cub." Nicole grabbed a large, meaty bone, and the two headed for the panther cage.

"*Pourquoi?*" Gabrielle asked. "You can't go in and help Josephine —it's too dangerous."

"I know," Nicole replied. "Remember that iron ladder on the side of the cage? When Josephine goes into labor, I'll climb the ladder and shoot Napoleon with a tranquilizer dart. It won't hurt him, but while he's asleep I can lure Josephine out of the holding area and safely remove her cub. In the past, every time Josephine and Napoleon have had a cub, Napoleon has killed it. He won't kill the new cub while I am on duty!"

Gabrielle pulled the handle that locked the panther out in its yard. Then her sister opened the zookeeper's door and the two started cleaning the holding area. Gabrielle could hear the big black cat purring loudly as it paced back and forth behind the door.

"What if Josephine delivers during the day when the bears are on exhibit?" Gabrielle asked. "Napoleon might kill the cub before you can do anything."

Nicole looked thoughtful. "I'm hoping she'll deliver her cub during the night, as she has before. If she goes into labor during the day, I'll close the exhibit and lock Napoleon out of the holding area."

"Why don't you just separate the bears until the cub grows up? It would be a lot easier."

Nicole smiled. Gabrielle's curiosity, and her seriousness about becoming a veterinarian, were the reasons Nicole had allowed Gabrielle to apprentice with her as an assistant zookeeper.

"I'm afraid Josephine won't take care of her baby if she's separated from Napoleon," Nicole explained. "She howls and moans any time we separate them. They have been together for sixteen years, and neither likes to be alone. In the wild it's different. After mating, a female bear hides from males in a snow den until her cub—or cubs—are three or four months old. Here that's impossible. Josephine's cub will have a better chance of surviving if it's raised by zookeepers."

Gabrielle smiled her sweetest smile at her sister. "Nicole? *S'il vous plaît...?*"

"Sorry, Gabrielle," Nicole interrupted. "I wish you could stay with me. But only employees can spend the night at the zoo. I'll call you if anything happens."

Gabrielle dragged her feet on the way home that evening. She had really wanted to be there when Josephine delivered her cub.

Two days passed, and still no cub was born. Gabrielle and Nicole were about to feed the polar bears when Nicole received an urgent page from the zoo's vet clinic. She looked anxiously into the polar bear cage. Napoleon slept comfortably on the concrete, his white muzzle on his paws. Promising to return as soon as possible, Nicole ran toward the clinic.

Gabrielle leaned against the exhibit railing and gazed in. To her right was the swimming pool; to her left the concrete yard with its many ledges where the bears climbed and sunned themselves. Gabrielle thought they looked like rocky cliffs. Straight ahead was the holding area with its large sliding door.

Gabrielle's stomach growled. Napoleon was still sleeping soundly, so she decided to buy a snack from a nearby vending machine. She had walked only a short distance when she heard angry howls coming from the polar bear yard. She ran back and saw Napoleon trying to push his way through the open holding area door.

Gabrielle sprinted behind the cage and looked through the zookeeper's door. She saw Napoleon growling fiercely, trying to push past Josephine into the holding area. Josephine was howling as she tried to block the doorway with her eight-hundred-pound body. Shrill cries came from the back of the holding area.

"The cries must be the newborn cub," Gabrielle thought. She had to do something. Nicole had said the only time Josephine and Napoleon fought was when Josephine delivered a cub and tried to protect it. Napoleon snapped at Josephine and inched forward.

"Oh, Nicole!" Gabrielle yelled. "Hurry back!" As Gabrielle looked around, she saw the hose they used to clean the yard. Gabrielle turned the hose on full blast, and aimed the stream at the bears. But the water just slid off the bears' fur and pooled on the ground.

"I wish Nicole was here with her tranquilizer gun," Gabrielle thought. "But I don't have time to wait."

Gabrielle grabbed the food bucket beside the zookeeper's door and ran to the side of the bears' cage. She climbed the iron ladder, gripping the ladder with one hand while pulling the heavy bucket up with the other. "Here, Napoleon! Feeding time!" she yelled as she dumped food into the yard. It didn't work. Either Napoleon didn't smell the food, or he cared a lot more about the smell of the newborn cub.

"What would get Napoleon's attention?" Gabrielle thought as Napoleon pushed further into the holding area. She screamed at him in frustration and Napoleon turned to investigate. She yelled and screamed some more, frantically waving her free arm. Napoleon watched for a moment, then returned to his attack against Josephine, who was weakening.

Gabrielle eyed the bucket in her hand. "If Napoleon was distracted by noise," she thought, "a tin bucket would make a lot more noise." Reaching over the wall as far as possible, Gabrielle threw the bucket into the cage. The bucket hit the concrete with a startling clang and clattered as it rolled about.

Two things happened at once: the force of the throw plunged Gabrielle forward, and both bears came out to investigate the noise.

As she fell, Gabrielle hooked her right foot under a rung of the ladder; Gabrielle shrieked as her ankle wrenched. She thudded against the wall, and found herself dangling upside down. Gabrielle knew if she fell to the ground, she'd be mauled by the two raging bears. She'd save the cub all right—at the cost of her own life. A few yards below her head, the polar bears growled menacingly at her.

"Nice bears!" Gabrielle crooned, willing herself not to panic. "Remember me? I'm the one who takes such good care of you."

Napoleon wasn't soothed. Standing on his hind feet, he swatted at Gabrielle with his massive paws. He barely missed, and Gabrielle wasn't going to wait around to see if he could get any closer.

Grimacing with determination, Gabrielle pushed herself up the wall. Her wrists and arms burned as if they'd snap, but she slowly inched her way up. Finally, she clutched the ladder with both hands and pulled herself back over the wall.

Shaking uncontrollably, Gabrielle climbed down the ladder. She jumped the last two feet to the ground and yelped when she landed on her hurt foot.

"No time to think about the pain," Gabrielle thought. Josephine was running to the holding area, with Napoleon right behind her. Gabrielle painfully limped around the cage and yanked the handle to close the holding area door. The door slid shut, locking Josephine and Napoleon outside.

Gabrielle collapsed in a heap against the wall, holding her aching sides and trying to steady her breath. Hot tears of relief slipped down her cheeks. Wiping the tears on the sleeve of her work jacket, Gabrielle muttered, "Being a veterinarian will be easy compared to being a zookeeper!"

"Gabbbrielle!" Nicole yelled. "Where are you?"

"Behind the holding area!" Gabrielle shouted.

Soon Nicole was squatting next to her sister as Gabrielle explained what had happened. When she finished, Nicole hugged her tightly. "I'm so glad you're all right," she said. "Throwing the bucket into the cage was a great idea. Napoleon hates loud noises."

A squeal grabbed their attention—the cub. Nicole unlocked the zookeeper's door and she and Gabrielle walked inside the holding area. In the hay piled in one corner squirmed a tiny, pink, hairless cub. Gabrielle gently lifted the cub, then gritted her teeth against the shooting pains in her ankle as she sat down. The cub was trembling, so she snuggled it against her.

"You sweet little thing," she crooned. "I didn't know you would be this tiny." The cub fit into the palms of Gabrielle's hands, and its eyes were closed. Before she knew it, it had found her finger and was contentedly sucking on it.

Nicole obtained permission to care for the cub at home until it could grow big enough to be moved back to the zoo. It needed special care and bottle feedings every hour-and-a-half to help it survive.

Because Gabrielle had saved the female cub's life, she was given the privilege of naming it, as well as helping her sister care for it. On Christmas morning, Gabrielle finally decided on a name. "I think I'll name her Noëlle. Because she was born in December."

Gabrielle became Noëlle's substitute mother, cuddling and feeding and playing with her until she was too big—and her claws and teeth too sharp—for Gabrielle to be safely in the cage with her anymore.

"One day I'll be a veterinarian and I'll take special care of you," Gabrielle promised Noëlle through the zookeeper's door. "Until then, here you go." She pushed Noëlle's favorite treat, a triple-decker ice-cream cone, through the bars. While Noëlle licked the ice cream, Gabrielle opened the door and petted the cub. Then she locked the door again with her very own key.

Tricking the Wolves

AN ORIGINAL STORY BY DOUGLAS C. DOSSON

Meriwa paused from her work and looked out across the snow-covered valley. An icy wind blowing from the north signaled that the brief Arctic summer had already left northern Canada. The women and children in the Inuit village were busily preparing for the harsh winter ahead. But with all of the men far away hunting caribou, the village seemed very lonely.

Meriwa's big sled dog, Mu, whined, and Meriwa knelt down to comfort him. Meriwa's father believed that Mu was now too old for the hunt and had left him behind when all the hunting sleds had pulled out of the village. Mu was not taking his rejection well and had been pacing and whining for several days.

Meriwa understood how Mu felt. She felt the same rejection each year when the hunters left her behind. She could drive a dog sled as well as any boy in her village, but Inuit tradition required the females to stay home and prepare for the arrival of the caribou meat, while the males went out to hunt the migrating herd.

Meriwa hugged Mu's big neck and stood up with a sigh. Her mother was very ill. Meriwa wanted very much to stay with her mother, but she had too much work to do. Instead Sedna, the village healer, was staying by her side. Sedna had promised Meriwa that she'd do all she could to help her mother.

Later that morning, Meriwa entered her family's cabin, hoping to see an improvement in her mother's condition. But when she stepped inside, she saw that it was worse. Meriwa sat silently in the flickering light of the oil lamp while her mother lay under a thick fur blanket, breathing heavily, too weak to even turn her head to look at her daughter. Meriwa fought back tears.

"Sedna," she said at last, "what will help my mother get better?"

"Nothing I have. Nothing I can make," Sedna said. "This sickness came from the white people, and it can only be healed by their medicine."

"Where can I get this medicine?" Meriwa asked.

"Only in Fort Reliance." Fort Reliance was the nearest town.

"Then I will go."

"No, Meriwa," Sedna said. "Our people are not welcome there."

"But I have the white people's money," Meriwa insisted, "and I have been to their town before."

"Oh, yes," Sedna said, "with your father and your cousins. But the men are on the hunt, and all the dogs are with them."

"Not all the dogs," Meriwa said. "Mu is here. Many of the other older dogs are here, too. They can take me to the town."

"Maybe so," said Sedna, "but the wolves are active now, hunting for food before the harsh weather comes. The men have all the rifles. How will you defend yourself against hungry wolves?"

Meriwa knew that Sedna was right. At the start of winter, Arctic wolves became very aggressive as they searched for food. They were even known to attack humans, whom they usually avoided.

Meriwa's mother moaned faintly. Despite her fear, Meriwa knew she must figure out some way to get through to the town. She hurried off to find Ahdik, the oldest man in the village. Although he was nearly blind now and rarely left the warmth of his fire, Ahdik had once been a great hunter. Meriwa hoped that he could tell her how to handle the wolves.

"Ahdik," Meriwa said respectfully as she entered the old man's cabin. "It is Meriwa. I must go to the white people's settlement for medicine to save my mother's life. I can handle the team and find the way, but I am afraid of the wolves and I have no rifle."

A mischievous smile lit Ahdik's face. "If you don't have a rifle, you'll have to use your wits," he said, "as we did before we had rifles."

"My wits?" she asked. "But how?"

"Wolves are fierce," Ahdik said. "But they are not clever. I know you are a clever girl, Meriwa. I will tell you how to trick the wolves."

Without hesitation, the old hunter explained how the Inuit used to trick the wolves in days gone by. Meriwa thanked Ahdik, then hurried to prepare for her journey, confident that she could succeed. She gathered the strongest of the elderly dogs and harnessed the team to Ahdik's old sled. She chose her own dog, Mu, to lead the team. As she harnessed him into his position, his tail wagged wildly. Meriwa guessed that he was as excited at the prospect of a journey as she was.

The news of Meriwa's adventure spread quickly. Women from every corner of the village brought things for her journey. One woman brought thick mittens. Another brought a warm blanket because Meriwa would have to spend the night on the trail. Several brought food, including dried fish for the dogs, who would be ravenous after a hard day's work. Last of all came Sedna, who handed Meriwa an empty brown medicine bottle with writing on it.

"Take this to the doctor's office," she said. "The person there will fill this bottle with the medicine your mother needs to live."

Meriwa thanked Sedna and tucked the bottle deep in the pocket of her parka. She was ready to go now.

"Mush!" she called to the eager dogs. As the sled sped away, Meriwa marveled, as she always did, at the dogs' grace and power.

The trail to the white people's town followed the river northwest. Although the trail was seldom used, it was clear enough for Meriwa's sled to skim smoothly on the freshly fallen snow. Mu responded to Meriwa's commands, leading the team flawlessly.

They traveled all day and crossed the river a mile north of the rapids, where the current under the ice moved slowly and there was a clear bank on the other side. The ice was dangerously thin, but Meriwa knew it was even thinner closer to the rapids.

"Faster, Mu!" Meriwa cried as the team slid onto the creaking ice. Meriwa held onto the runners of the sled, scrambling to keep up and not fall through the holes that were breaking open behind her with every step.

At last they were safely on the other side. They clambered up the riverbank and continued along the trail. Meriwa glanced over her shoulder. There was a path of broken ice across the river, but fortunately she was still dry, and everything on the sled was, too.

It was then that Meriwa saw the fresh tracks crossing her trail. The wolves had been here recently. Although they were nowhere to be seen, Meriwa mentally rehearsed her plan for tricking the wolves.

It was nearly too dark to see the trail when Meriwa made camp. She groomed the dogs and gave them a well-deserved supper of dried fish. After eating, the dogs dug beds in the shallow snow and huddled together. However, Meriwa gave Mu a special place behind her in the sled—partly to reward him for his good work and partly to keep her warm through the frigid night. Meriwa listened to the eerie howling of the wolves, many miles away, but she was too tired to worry about them now. She drifted off to sleep thinking of her poor mother and the important brown bottle in her pocket.

Early the next morning, Meriwa fed and harnessed the dogs and started off. Two hours later she pulled into Fort Reliance. It was still quite early and no people were out on the street. Meriwa was glad. She didn't want to attract any attention. Meriwa drove right to the doctor's office in the center of town, hitched the dogs to a light pole, and marched inside.

"This, please," Meriwa said, placing the bottle on the counter.

A woman in white came to the counter and examined the bottle carefully. "Do you have money?" she asked suspiciously.

Meriwa pulled a small wad of dollar bills from the pocket of her parka. The lady looked surprised, but quickly refilled the bottle.

"Se-ven dol-lars," she said slowly, pronouncing every letter as if Meriwa wouldn't understand unless she said it that way.

"You don't have to talk like that," Meriwa said firmly. "I can speak English." With that, she laid seven dollars on the counter and picked up the precious bottle of medicine. "Thank you," she said with a smile.

"You're quite welcome," the lady responded, and for the first time she smiled, too. Meriwa felt more confident as she left the doctor's office and returned to her sled.

The team seemed anxious to get back on the trail, so Meriwa put the bottle in her pocket and stepped onto the sled. She knew the dogs would move faster now with the north wind at their backs, and the ice on the river would be thicker after the cold night.

Meriwa and her team made good time to the rapids, then easily crossed the river. The north wind didn't feel so icy once they were deep in the woods, and the musical yelping of the sled dogs made

Meriwa happy and proud. She was sure that she would get the medicine to her mother on time.

Suddenly, Meriwa spotted movement out of the corner of her eye. She sensed danger and she knew the dogs did, too. But several minutes passed before the wolves showed themselves. They kept pace with the team about a hundred feet away in the timbers. Meriwa could see five wolves. Their big heads and slender bodies made them look hungry and scary. Meriwa hoped that Ahdik's trick would work.

She called for Mu to speed up. She knew her old dogs could never outrun the wolves, but her plan required pulling ahead of them for a brief time. She saw a big fir tree ahead and urged the dogs to run as fast as they could. She stopped the sled right under the tree and quickly unharnessed old Mu. He couldn't last long in a fight with the wolves, but the veteran sled dog knew how to hold them at bay.

Mu went right to work, growling and snarling at the rear of the sled while the wolves paused to size him up. Meanwhile, Meriwa drew her knife and frantically chipped a small hole in a frozen puddle at the base of the fir. Then she pulled one arm out of her parka and grabbed all of the remaining dried fish. She shoved the fish into the hole and as far back under the ice as her slender arm could reach.

"Come, Mu," she called as she thrust her arm back into its sleeve. She latched him back into his harness as the other dogs fidgeted.

"Now mush!" she cried, and again they were off. Meriwa looked back. The wolves couldn't resist the food lodged under the ice, but the hole was too small for them to get at it easily. The wolves would have to paw at the ice for hours to reach the fish. Meriwa and her team would be long gone by the time they did. "Wolves are fierce, but they are not clever," Meriwa repeated with a smile.

With the dangerous wolves behind them now, Meriwa and her team finished the trail in good spirits. They arrived at the village just as it was turning dark. Meriwa hurried to her cabin and found old Sedna still at her mother's bedside.

Meriwa passed the precious bottle to the skilled healer without saying a word.

"You have done well, Meriwa," Sedna said with an approving nod. "Now your mother will live."

When the hunters finally returned to the village, the success of their hunt was overshadowed by the exciting story of Meriwa's lifesaving journey. And to this day her story is still told and retold among the Inuit whenever an elder asks a child to "use her wits."

To Catch a Cat

An Original Story by Patricia Russo

Spanish Words:

Mamá (pronounced "ma-MA"): means "mother."

Galletas (pronounced "gal-LE-tas"): means "cookies."

Hola (pronounced "o-LA"): means "hello."

Pequeñino (pronounced "pe-que-NI-no"): means "little one."

Snow was falling lightly in Newark when Mercedes got out of school. She tugged down the hood of her jacket, but the cold wet flakes still plastered themselves across her cheeks. She wished Luisa would hurry up. Ever since they'd met in kindergarten five years ago, Luisa had walked home with Mercedes and stayed there until her *mamá* got off work.

Luisa came running out the school door, still zipping up her coat. She nearly dropped her books as she skidded on the icy cement. "Let's go before we freeze," she said. Mercedes smiled at her friend. Luisa hated cold weather.

Mercedes and Luisa crossed the street and took a shortcut through a gas station. As the girls passed the boarded-up house on the corner of Newark Avenue, Mercedes turned her face away. She hated that old house, with its peeling paint and missing shingles. It made her feel sad and hollow inside.

Suddenly Luisa stopped dead. "Mercedes, look! It's still there."

The house had been empty since the Galindez family moved away last April. They'd loaded up two trucks with their beds and dressers and chairs, but they'd forgotten one thing—their cat. Mercedes had a nasty suspicion that they hadn't forgotten at all...that they'd left the little gray cat behind on purpose.

The cat crouched on the cracked sidewalk in front of the boarded-up house. The cat was so skinny that Mercedes could see its ribs under its short fur. The cat's yellow-green eyes seemed huge in its drawn face.

Mercedes and Luisa had seen the cat all summer, sitting on the steps or lying on the sidewalk. They'd last seen it more than a month ago. Now the cat was back, dirtier and skinnier than ever, still waiting for its people to come home and open the door.

"The poor thing is starving," Luisa cried, moving toward him. In a flash, the cat fled to the top of the steps. It crouched there, swishing his tail fearfully.

"Wait," Mercedes said. "Don't scare it away."

But Luisa ran toward the steps anyway. The cat hissed, leaped off the top step, and landed on the ground five feet below with a thud. Then it ran around the side of the wooden steps and vanished.

"Where'd it go?" Mercedes asked.

"In there," Luisa said, pointing.

There was a storage area under the front steps that was secured with a padlocked wooden gate. One of the bottom slats of the gate was missing, leaving a gap that the skinny gray cat could fit through easily.

The snow was coming down harder. White flakes stuck to Mercedes's coat, and dusted Luisa's hair like talcum powder. "Come on," Luisa said. "I'm freezing."

"So's the cat," Mercedes said sadly.

At Mercedes's house, Mercedes and Luisa ignored the plate of *galletas* Mercedes's mother had set out on the kitchen table. As soon as they'd sat down, Mercedes's cat, Pepita, jumped into Luisa's lap. Luisa stroked her, and she started to purr. Pepita was a marmalade cat, mostly orange with speckles of brown. She was big and warm and sweet-tempered. Pepita loved everybody.

Mercedes looked at Pepita and her throat grew tight. Pepita had a warm home and food and people to love her. The little gray cat had none of these things.

Mercedes's mother was listening to the radio with a worried expression on her face. "Did you hear that?" she asked. "A blizzard is coming."

"It's snowing already, *Mamá*," Mercedes said.

Mercedes and Luisa looked at each other.

"What is it?" Mercedes's mother asked.

"We saw the Galindez's cat again," Mercedes said, "It's still waiting for them to come home."

Mercedes's mother bit her lip. "They're predicting three feet of snow."

"*Mamá*, if I catch the cat, can I bring him home?"

"I don't know," her mother said slowly.

"It'll die, Mrs. Rivera," Luisa said, her voice trembling. "The cat's so skinny. I don't think it's eaten for days."

Mercedes could see her mother wavering, so she ran to fetch Pepita's carrying case. Her mother sighed. "All right," she said. "But listen to me carefully. Catch the cat if you can, but I don't want either of you petting it or playing with it until a vet says it's okay."

"Yes, *Mamá*," Mercedes promised. She took a can of Pepita's food from the pantry shelf.

The girls hurried to the abandoned house. When they reached the corner, Mercedes sighed with relief. The little gray cat was lying on the top step. Luisa set the carrying case on the sidewalk and tugged the door open. The cat eyed the girls warily.

"*Hola, pegueñino,*" Mercedes said. "Hi, little one. Don't be scared." The cat laid its ears flat and tensed its muscles. Mercedes popped the can's lid and peeled it back, then waved her hand to waft the scent of cat food toward the steps.

"Mmmrrrew," the little gray cat said weakly, pricking up its ears. It stared at the can.

"It's interested," Luisa said.

Mercedes rose slowly and walked toward the steps, holding the can out enticingly. "Here, little guy. Come on. Here, kitty-kitty. Nice food."

"Mmmmmrrrrrow."

Her heart pounding, Mercedes put one foot on the bottom step. The cat stood up, but didn't flee. Mercedes mounted the second step. She was almost within arm's reach. She put her foot on the third step, then set the can on the top step. The cat flinched, but the smell of food was too strong for it to resist. The cat leaned forward and warily licked the cat food in the can.

"Good kitty," Mercedes whispered, easing closer.

The cat jerked its head up, hissing fiercely. Bunching its wasted muscles, the cat leaped off the steps and disappeared under the broken gate again.

Mercedes walked down the steps and set the open can in front of the gap in the gate. "Maybe it'll come back out."

The girls waited, hopefully at first. Then the afternoon darkened, and before long snow began to fall again. The little cat never came out. When they went back indoors, Mercedes's mother hugged her. "You didn't get the cat?"

"No. It wouldn't come. It was too scared."

"The cat's been on its own for a long time," Mercedes's mother said. "It probably doesn't trust people anymore."

"Except the Galindezes," Mercedes thought, "and they don't deserve his trust. They left him behind like a broken toaster."

Luisa set down the empty carrying case. She was blinking hard.

"Luisa, would you like to stay for dinner?" Mercedes's mother asked.

"Yes, thank you," Luisa said, blinking even harder.

"Go call your mother, then." As Luisa left the room, Mercedes's mother kissed the top of Mercedes's head. "Never mind. You did your best."

But Mercedes did mind. She wanted to cry at the thought of that little cat out alone in the cold. "The cat didn't come to us because it didn't trust us," Mercedes thought. "Food isn't enough to lure it out of hiding. If we just had some way to show the cat that it could trust us."

Mercedes's mother looked out the window. "Poor cat," she murmured. "The snow's really coming down."

Pepita jumped on the chair beside them and rubbed her head against Mercedes's arm. Mercedes stroked her, and Pepita purred loudly. When Luisa came back into the kitchen, she watched Mercedes rubbing Pepita. "The gray cat's going to die, isn't it?" she asked.

"Girls, you tried," Mercedes's mother said. "There's nothing more you can do."

"The cat didn't trust us," Mercedes said. "That's why it ran away." Suddenly she stopped stroking Pepita. An idea glimmered in her mind. "Pepita trusts us," she said. "Maybe the little gray cat would trust us if Pepita showed it how."

Luisa stared at her. Mercedes yanked on her coat and hat, then scooped Pepita into her arms.

"I don't know," her mother said. "It's getting pretty dark out."

"Please, *Mamá*. Please let us try."

Luisa grabbed the carrying case. "Please, Mrs. Rivera. This is the cat's last chance!"

"All right," Mercedes's mother said, throwing her hands up. "But I want you back here in fifteen minutes, cat or no cat."

The girls hurried through the falling snow to the boarded-up house. Mercedes held Pepita tight to her chest.

"Look! It's on the step!" Luisa cried.

So it was, huddled in a miserable ball. Its eyes were shut, and for a horrible moment Mercedes thought the cat was dead. Then it opened its eyes and streaked down the steps, vanishing through the gap in the gate.

"The can's empty," Luisa said. "At least it ate."

"Get the carrying case ready," Mercedes said.

Mercedes sat down next to the empty can. The snow was already a couple of inches deep, but she didn't care. Pepita didn't care, either. She sat calmly in Mercedes's lap. Mercedes petted her, and Pepita purred, kneading Mercedes's leg with her paws. The more Mercedes petted Pepita, the louder the cat purred.

A little whiskered nose peeped out from under the broken gate. It twitched. Then a skinny gray face poked out. Mercedes kept stroking Pepita, and Pepita kept purring.

The little gray cat inched all the way onto the sidewalk. It stared as if it were struggling to recall distant memories of affection like this. The cat padded toward Mercedes and Pepita, hesitated, then approached again.

Purring loudly, Pepita sniffed the little gray cat's nose, then licked its chin. The gray cat meowed softly.

Slowly, Mercedes reached out one finger and touched the cat lightly on its back. It stiffened, but didn't move away. She ran her finger down the cat's back—once, twice, three times—until it relaxed. Mercedes let her gloved hand rest on the cat's back for a moment, then eased her hand down to its belly.

"Luisa," she called softly.

Luisa crept forward with the carrying case. With one quick motion, Mercedes scooped the cat up and popped it inside the case. The cat hissed as Luisa snapped the door shut. Pepita never stopped purring.

"We did it!" Luisa cried. "Come on, let's get home. It's freezing out here!"

When the vet checked out the little cat, she said he was underweight but healthy.

"Can we keep him, *Mamá*?" Mercedes asked.

"Oh, I think so. I'd say you earned him, Mercedes!"

Mercedes looked at Luisa. "You earned him as much as me. He's half yours now."

Luisa grinned. "I'll be over so much you'll get sick of me."

"No, I won't," Mercedes said, grinning back.

Suddenly, Luisa burst out laughing. Mercedes and her mother looked at Luisa, puzzled. "What's so funny?" Mercedes asked.

"Look. Pepita thinks she's his *mamá*. I guess he doesn't belong to either of us!"

They all looked, then laughed. Pepita had the little gray cat pinned down with her paws and was licking him from head to tail. And the little gray cat looked like he didn't mind it at all.

Rachel's War

AN ORIGINAL STORY BY MARTHA JOHNSON

Boston. March, 1775.

"Rachel Anne Welbourne! Come here immediately and help with the serving." Aunt Elizabeth's shrill voice penetrated the pantry door. Rachel squeezed behind a barrel of flour and held her breath.

She should have picked a better hiding place. The British officers who lived at her aunt's boarding house were just sitting down to dinner. Her aunt might hurry into the pantry at any moment and find her.

Aunt Elizabeth didn't understand how Rachel hated living in a house full of strangers. Aunt

Elizabeth had never been shy a day in her life. "The world has enough chatterboxes," Papa always said. Aunt Elizabeth didn't agree. When Rachel blushed and stammered, Aunt Elizabeth thought Rachel was being naughty.

Besides, Rachel couldn't serve British officers. She just couldn't. Not when the British had closed the port of Boston and filled the city with redcoats. Not when her own father and brother were drilling with the Minutemen in Roxbury, across the Boston Neck, and talk of liberty was everywhere.

Footsteps sounded in the hall. Rachel scrunched backward, heart pounding. The cupboard behind the flour barrel was just big enough to hold an eleven-year-old. She squirmed inside, sending a puff of loose flour that floated in the air. She held back a sneeze.

Suddenly, the pantry door swung open and Aunt Elizabeth's impatient steps crossed the room. Rachel pressed against the back wall. For a moment her aunt's foot tapped, then she whirled with a rustle of skirts and was gone.

Rachel breathed again. If her aunt had found her, she'd have been—

"… teach those rebels a lesson this time."

Rachel jumped, smacking her head on the shelf. Then she realized the voice came from the dining room, which was on the other side of the wall behind her. She pressed her ear to the rough plaster. It was Lieutenant Armistead speaking, one of her aunt's guests.

"All their drilling will be worthless once we seize the weapons they've been collecting." Lieutenant Armistead's voice sounded satisfied. "By tomorrow night we'll have cleaned every musket and every speck of powder from that barn near Roxbury. Those Minutemen will be drilling with broomsticks when we're done."

Rachel's blood ran cold as the officers laughed. The barn they spoke of was her father's barn! The British were going to raid it!

Rachel scrambled from the cupboard and squeezed past the flour barrel. Her mind was racing faster than her pounding heart. Papa had to be warned. But how could she reach him?

Jonathan Martin. He was one of the Sons of Liberty. He could be trusted with such an important message. She'd slip out while her aunt was busy in the dining room, hurry around the corner to Jonathan's house, give him the message, and—

"There you are!" Aunt Elizabeth's fingers pinched on Rachel's ear. "Where do you think you're going, young lady?"

Two hours later, Rachel finished scrubbing the last of the pots. The tinkling of harpsichord music told her that her aunt was in the parlor. She glanced toward the kitchen door. To get the message to Jonathan in time, she'd have to go now, before Aunt Elizabeth chased her off to bed.

She tiptoed across the room and lifted her cloak from its peg. Easing the door open, she slipped out into the darkness of the kitchen garden.

Rachel shivered as she hurried down the cobblestone street. She hadn't been outside at night since her father sent her to stay with her aunt. It wasn't suitable, Aunt Elizabeth said, for a young lady to run about. Aunt Elizabeth had all sorts of rules for proper conduct, and Rachel seemed to break most of them.

A fierce longing to be back on the farm with Papa and her brother, Ben, swept through her, cold as the March wind.

"These are dangerous times, Rachel-girl," her father had said as she'd packed her trunk for Boston. "The fighting could start at any moment."

"But I want to stay, Papa. I can help."

Ben had patted her shoulder. "It won't be long till we beat those redcoats. Then you can come home again." His round cheeks flushed, and from behind his back he pulled out his blue kite. "Take this with you. You can fly it on the hill above Aunt Elizabeth's house."

"Your best kite!" Rachel had blinked back tears. "You shouldn't give me that. I have the red one we made."

"You don't want to fly that ugly thing," Ben had said. "It looks like a British war banner. Fly the blue one every Sunday—I'll watch for it. When you see my striped kite, you'll know we're all right."

Rachel had stowed the kite carefully in her trunk, hoping Ben hadn't seen the tears in her eyes.

He'd grasped her shoulder tightly for a moment. "You'll have to be careful with those redcoats in Boston, Rachel. But I'm sure you'll be safe."

Now, Rachel wished she felt as sure of that as Ben had. She hurried around the corner, rehearsing the words she'd say to Jonathan. She had to make him understand how important her message was.

She stopped dead, her heart pounding. Soldiers filled the street outside Jonathan's house. In the midst of them was Jonathan! Wrists shackled, he stumbled as one of the soldiers pushed him.

Rachel shrank back, but it was too late. One of the soldiers swung around, spotted her, and grabbed her arm.

"What are you doing here, girl? Speak up!"

Rachel's stomach flipped. Blood rushed to her cheeks. "I… I…"

His grip tightened. "What's the matter? Cat got your tongue?"

Her words stuck in her throat. Suddenly an officer snapped an order. The soldier released her and joined the group around Jonathan. They marched off down the street. As the clack of their soles on the cobblestones faded, Rachel began to relax.

How would she warn Papa now? If Papa didn't know about the attack, he could be arrested, like Jonathan. A picture of Papa and Ben trying to defend the barn against soldiers formed in her head, and she felt sick. They could be hurt—or killed!

There was only one thing to do. She'd have to deliver the warning herself. She knew the way, of course. Hadn't she stood in the field near Aunt Elizabeth's house and looked across the water, seeing the hill above her father's farm? She could picture the narrow strip of land, the Boston Neck, that led toward Roxbury, and home.

A click of heels on the cobblestones sent Rachel scurrying into the nearest doorway. She flattened herself against the door as a red-coated sentry strolled by. She'd have to be careful. Anyone who saw her would wonder why an eleven-year-old girl was out alone at night.

Two blocks, three, four...Rachel hurried along, ducking into the shadows each time she heard footsteps. Why were so many soldiers out tonight? She imagined they knew the secret she carried. Rachel shivered as a chill breeze whistled down the street, whipping her cloak around her. By this time, Aunt Elizabeth had probably discovered she was missing. Rachel quickened her steps.

"Hold on there!"

Rachel froze at the shout that echoed in the quiet street behind her. Should she run? Could she outrace a British soldier? If there was only the one behind her...her heart thumped as a figure stepped in front of her. The white stitching on his red coat reflected the moonlight.

"Well, now," he said, reaching for her. "Looks like we've caught ourselves a runaway."

Rachel hung her head as the soldiers took her back to Aunt Elizabeth's house. She'd failed. The raiding party would leave in the morning. The soldiers would find the Minutemen's weapons, and if her father and Ben tried to resist... Rachel closed her mind against that thought.

"Rachel!" Aunt Elizabeth hugged her fiercely, then just as fiercely she shook Rachel. "How could you do such a thing, you wicked girl? Whatever would your father say?"

"Surely it's not as bad as all that, Mistress Morgan." Lieutenant Armistead said, stepped out of the house, followed by another officer. "Young Rachel was just looking for adventure, I'll wager." He smiled at Rachel, then bowed to her aunt and strode down the steps.

"I say, Armistead, what's your hurry?" the other officer asked. "We'll be lucky to leave Boston by midafternoon, the way Colonel Smith dallies."

His words rang in Rachel's ears. Midafternoon. That meant she hadn't failed after all! She still had time to get a warning to her father. But how? She looked up and nearly cried out in frustration. If only she could fly over the Boston Neck, up the hill—like a bird, like a kite.

As the idea came to her, Rachel barely heard Aunt Elizabeth's scolding. She had one last chance to get the warning out. And she knew exactly what to do.

Rachel slept fitfully that night. She got up while it was still dark, so she could be ready to slip out at first light. At sunrise, Rachel arrived in the meadow above Aunt Elizabeth's house. Below her, she could see soldiers assembling on the Common, and her heart thumped at the sight of those red coats. Carefully, she smoothed out the red kite, the one Ben thought was so ugly. The one he'd said looked like a British war banner.

She straightened the tail of the kite. She wouldn't let herself think that Ben might not see it, or might not remember what he'd said and understand her warning. This was her only chance. It had to work. She knew Ben would be awake, bustling about the farmyard, tending to the animals. He had only to look up towards Boston.

The March wind that had gusted all night had died. The air was leaden, unwilling to help. Puffy clouds dotted the sky. Rachel thought of everything she and Ben knew about launching a kite. There wasn't much wind and she had no one to help her. She'd have to run with it and hope to catch a breeze.

She ran, red kite held high in one hand, stumbling on the clumpy, brown winter grass. As her feet and heart pounded, she felt the kite lift. She let it go. It crashed to the ground and lay there like a stone.

Tears welled in her eyes, but she couldn't give up. She tried one more time, telling herself to check the wind, run, and wait…wait…wait until she could feel a faint breeze. Now!

Rachel released the kite. It caught the wind! She played out the string, letting the kite soar higher and higher. Rachel's spirits lifted with the kite. Surely anyone looking would notice it. But was anyone looking? She strained her eyes toward the hill above her family's farm. "Please, Ben," she thought. "Please look this way. Please understand." She played out the line, letting the kite climb higher, until she'd nearly reached the end of the string.

"What are you doing, girl?" Rachel jerked toward the gruff voice. Her heart pounded. A redcoat stood behind her. "Well?" he said. "What's wrong? Speak up."

The lump in her throat felt bigger than the kite. Her cheeks burned, and her tongue seemed too thick to speak. But if she didn't speak, what would the soldier do? He might take her kite away, thinking she was hiding something.

Rachel pictured Papa's face, felt Ben's hand on her shoulder. She swallowed hard. "I… I… I'm just flying my kite." She needed another moment or two. Every minute she kept the kite in the air improved the chances that Ben would see it. Somehow she had to keep talking, even if the words tried to strangle her. "Nothing wrong with that, is there?"

The soldier frowned. Rachel's mind raced. If Ben were here, he'd think up an excuse quick as a wink. Ben had a ready answer for everything. But he wasn't here, and everything was up to Rachel. "One of the officers admired it," she said. "I'm flying it to wish him well; that's all."

For an instant she thought her excuse had worked. Then the soldier shook his head. "Sorry, lass. I'll have to pull it down."

He reached for the string. As his fingers opened to take it from her, Rachel let the string go. It fluttered, then rose. The soldier grabbed for it, but a puff of wind took the kite and the string danced away from his hand. It quickly lifted well above their heads.

"My kite!" Rachel managed to exclaim. "You lost my kite!"

The soldier clenched his jaw, and he glared up at the bright red kite. Rachel held her breath. Would he guess she'd deliberately let go of it?

"Sorry," the soldier muttered. "Too bad." He spun and stamped off across the meadow.

Finally she could turn and look. Had she done it? Had she kept the kite up long enough? Her gaze traveled across the water, toward home. Her breath caught in her throat. Ben's striped kite lifted into the sky. Even as she watched, it swooped up and down, as if nodding to her. As if saying, "Yes, I understand."

Rachel wiped tears away as she watched the kites dancing with each other high in the spring air. Ben and Papa would be safe. By the time the British reached the barn, they'd find only cows and hay— not muskets.

One day her family would be together again, and she'd tell Papa and Ben about how she'd found her voice. One day this terrible war would be over, and they'd be as free as the red kite, dancing on the wind.

Anna's Mystery

AN ORIGINAL STORY BY SHERYL LAWRENCE

Anna Doughty woke to the new baby's crying—as usual. There wasn't much light in her room yet, so she put the pillow over her head and tried to fall back asleep. Right. Who could sleep with all that noise?

Anna threw back her plaid comforter in exasperation and walked down the hall to her baby brother's room. Her frown disappeared as soon as she saw his little red face all scrunched up.

"Billy, why did you have to wake me up? This is my first day of summer vacation. I was hoping to sleep in. Shhhh…it's all right. I'll take you to Mama."

As she took Billy to her mother's room, she wondered whether he was why her dad had left. Maybe Dad couldn't stand crying babies. Maybe he was planning to come back when Billy was older. But she had been a baby once, and he hadn't left then. That couldn't be it. She'd have to keep thinking. This was one big mystery that she had to solve.

"Mom, your dirty-diaper machine is awake. He smells like he's been busy."

"H'mm?" Mom raised her head, hair sticking out in every direction and only one eye open. "Oh, no. I was up with him all night. He just went to sleep!"

Anna handed Billy over to Mom, then passed her the diaper bag. "Thanks, sweetie," Mom said.

"Want me to start the coffee?"

"That would be great. But only half a pot, okay?"

Half a pot. Dad used to drink the other half. Did he leave because Mom looked like Medusa in the morning, with snakes sprouting out of her head? Then a makeover was in order. She'd look through Mom's magazines for ideas.

"On second thought," Mom said, "never mind. You go on back to bed. It's summer vacation, after all. I'll wake you at ten so you can go and help Mrs. Kettering get ready for her trip."

Anna had forgotten that Mrs. K. was going away. She had called the older woman next door Mrs. K. ever since Anna was in kindergarten, and her family had moved to Toronto.

After climbing back into bed, Anna put herself to sleep by making up a mystery story: "The Case of the Missing Dad." Where had he gone and why?

The next thing Anna knew Mom was waking her up. "Upsy Daisy. Time for you to rise and shine."

Anna opened her eyes slowly. "I let you sleep late," Mom said. "It's 10:30. Come on, breakfast's ready."

Anna ate quickly, then hurried next door. Mrs. K. was going on a trip, and needed Anna's help to take Sasha, her cat, to the vet for boarding. Mrs. K. had a cat carrier, but Sasha hated being locked in it. She would hiss and yowl the whole time. Mrs. K. didn't like Sasha to be upset, so Anna would hold Sasha while Mrs. K. drove to the vet.

In the car, Mrs. K. talked excitedly about her trip. She was going to her nursing class reunion in Vancouver, and would ride a train for several days to get there. "That way I can see the countryside along the way," she said.

Anna wondered if Dad had taken a train.

The trip to the vet went fine. After saying good-bye to Sasha, they started back. They were almost home when Mrs. K. said, "The taxi will pick me up at five in the morning, so I have to get to bed early tonight."

"Why don't you drive your car to the train station?"

"Parking at the station is expensive. Besides, I'll feel better knowing my car is right here in my driveway rather than downtown."

"Have a fun time with your friends, Mrs. K."

"I'll bring you a souvenir."

"Okay, but no bedpans."

The next morning Anna slept in again. She woke up when her room was filled with light and realized that Mom must have gotten Billy up this morning. As she dressed, Anna hoped that Mrs. K. had caught her train.

Anna ate breakfast, then finished her latest mystery book. Mom went out to mow the lawn and asked her to listen for the baby. A little while later, Anna thought she heard Billy wake from his nap and crept into his room to check. He wasn't even stirring. Running her hand over the ABCs she'd helped stencil onto the walls, Anna wandered around the room, half-hoping Billy would wake up. She didn't have another book, and Mom didn't let her watch daytime television.

Anna looked out Billy's window, the one that faced Mrs. K.'s house. The house was small and neat, just like Mrs. K. Anna gazed absentmindedly at the flowers in the window boxes and the neatly drawn blinds.

Then she saw it. No, her eyes must be playing tricks on her. Mrs. K. was gone. Even if she were home, why would she open and shut the blinds like that?

"Look!" she shrieked. "There it is again!" Billy woke up and began to wail. "It's okay, Billy. Just your silly sister. Shhh, hold on. I've got to see something."

But Billy kept howling, making it hard for Anna to think. "Okay, Billy, what could it mean?" she asked, lifting him out of his crib. "Burglars? Then why mess with the blinds? Maybe it's a signal?"

Anna moved back to the window and resumed her watch while jiggling her brother. "What room is it?" she thought. "Let's see, if I walk in Mrs. K.'s door and go all the way to the right, I'd go through the living room, down the hall, and into the bathroom. That's it! But why would a crook waste time in the bathroom?"

Still wailing, Billy began winding his fingers in Anna's hair. She was watching the blinds too intently to notice. She tried not to blink, afraid she would miss another signal. Her eyes started to burn. Still no signal. Finally, she had to blink.

"Billy, did you see anything? Did I miss it?"

Billy's screaming turned shrill.

"Oh, not now, Billy. Mrs. K. could be in trouble."

"What's going on?" Anna hadn't heard Mom come inside. "Anna, what's wrong with Billy?"

Anna turned toward the door. "Mom, come here. I was watching Mrs. K.'s blinds, and I saw something."

"Poor baby, come to Mama. Oh, it's all right."

"Mrs. K.'s in trouble, Mom. She's trying to tell us she needs help. We've got to call the police or something. There might be an escaped prisoner over there who locked her in the bathroom or something. It must be serious, because she wouldn't miss her reunion for anything."

"Anna, that's enough," Mom snapped. "There is no mystery next door. I heard Mrs. Kettering leave this morning. The cab driver pulled up and honked the horn, then I heard a car door and footsteps. So enough of this nonsense. It's fun to see mysteries everywhere, but sometimes you have to get serious."

Anna and Mom spent the rest of the afternoon and evening quietly. They made dinner together, ate with the radio on, then cleaned up the kitchen. It was nearly eleven o'clock when Billy fell asleep in Mom's lap.

"I'll take him up, Mom. You relax."

"Thanks, sweetie."

As Anna covered Billy with his baby quilt, she saw Mrs. K.'s bathroom light showing through the open blinds. "Weren't they closed before?" Anna thought. "Why would she go away for a week and leave that light on?" Mrs. K. shut off lights every time she left a room. It was a joke between them how many times she had turned off a light while Anna was still in the room. "Oops," Mrs. K. would say. "I'll turn it back on."

Yet Mom had heard the taxi beep, heard the car door and footsteps. Wait—that wasn't right. Something about that didn't sound right at all.

Anna tore down the stairs. "Mom, that's not right."

Mom stood up, alarmed. "What's wrong? Is it Billy?"

"Mom, listen to me carefully. I'm not playing around. I think Mrs. K. is in trouble. Now, you said you heard the taxi honking, then the car door, then footsteps. It should have been the other way around. The footsteps, then the car door."

"Anna, what are you talking about? I—"

"Mom, her bathroom light is on. You know how she is about lights."

"Honey, old people can get absentminded. I myself forget things all the time."

"If Mrs. K. had come out after the cab honked, you would have heard the horn, then footsteps, then the car door. Think hard, Mom. What did you hear? Maybe the driver honked and no one came out, so he walked up and rang the door bell? Could it have been honk, car door, footsteps, car door again?"

"I…I'm not sure. Let me think."

"Most accidents happen at home. We learned that in fifth grade, Mom. And most of them happen in the bathtub. I think Mrs. K. has had an accident."

"Okay, okay. Let's go check. Let me get my shoes on. We'll leave the door open so we can listen for Billy."

"Hurry, Mom, hurry."

"I am, honey. Stay calm. It may be nothing."

As they crossed the yard, Anna could hear her mother muttering, "Let's see. Honk, steps…no, honk, door. Oh, now I'm not sure."

"That's all right, Mom. Let's just find out what's going on." When they reached Mrs. K.'s porch, Anna knocked hard on the door while her mother rang the bell. "Mrs. K., you in there? Hey, are you okay?"

"Mrs. Kettering, are you okay? Do you need help?"

They tried the front door, then the back. Both were locked. And the only sounds were passing cars and their own voices. They even checked the bathroom window. It was very high, so Mom gave

Anna a boost up. Anna rapped on the glass with her knuckles until they hurt, but she couldn't get a good look at anything except the ceiling.

"Honey, I don't think she's here."

"No, Mom. I can't give up until we know for sure."

"Anna, I understand how you feel. I really do. But how can we know? Are we going to break a window?"

"Mom, she may be counting on us to help her. What would Sasha do without her? Sasha! Mom, that's it."

"What? What's it?"

"I think I'm small enough to go in Sasha's door. Come on!"

Anna ran around the side of the house to the back door, and her mother followed. There it was: a small hole in the bottom of the door covered with a rubber flap so Sasha could come and go whenever she pleased. Anna was halfway through the cat door before her mother came around the corner.

"Be careful, Anna."

"It's all right, Mom. I can make it."

Once inside, Anna felt for the lock above the doorknob and turned it. Mom came in and flipped on lights as she walked to the bathroom, calling out, "Ruth, are you in here? Hello?"

Anna followed, content to let Mom take the lead now that she had gotten them inside. As Anna approached the bathroom, she heard Mom inhale sharply. Mrs. K. must be in there.

"Anna, I want you to be very calm and walk to the phone. Call 911, and tell them an elderly woman has taken a fall."

As Anna picked up the phone, she watched Mom enter the bathroom and lean over. She could hear Mom's voice; it was the voice Mom used with Billy. Then Anna was busy with the emergency dispatcher.

When she finally saw Mrs. K., Anna was sure that she was dead and started to cry. Mom looked over her shoulder and realized what Anna was thinking.

"She's in shock, honey, but she's alive. I think her hip is broken. Run out to the end of the driveway and flag down the ambulance."

Anna ran out to the road. She could already hear the siren. As the paramedics loaded Mrs. K. into the ambulance a few minutes later, Anna said, "Mom, go with her. I'll stay with Billy. Don't let her go alone."

It was almost a week before Mrs. K. was allowed visitors at the hospital. Anna was a little nervous about seeing her, but Mom said Mrs. Kettering looked much better now and wanted to see Anna. Mom sat in the lobby with Billy while Anna walked to Mrs. K.'s room.

As Anna stepped into the room, she was relieved to see that Mrs. K. was indeed looking better. "Knock, knock. Hi, Mrs. K. How are you doing?"

"Anna! Oh, I'm so happy to see you. I've been waiting to say this: you saved my life. You're such a clever girl. Come over here where I can hug you."

Anna walked to the bed, blushing. "Aw, geez, Mrs. K. I'm just glad you're okay. I wish I'd figured things out earlier."

Anna let herself be hugged and patted, but she was careful not to jiggle the bed or move Mrs. K.

"I was lying there for I don't know how long, just feeling helpless and cold, when I realized what I had to do. It took all my strength to hoist myself up and turn the wand for the blinds. I only managed it a few times, and I didn't think it would be noticeable during the day. After dark, I turned the wand once more, to leave the blinds open so you could see the light. Then I passed out. But you saw my signal, just as I knew you would. Now I need you to do something else for me."

"Sure, Mrs. K. What is it?"

"I'm going to stay with my daughter's family in Montreal for a while. They have a little room in their house that is perfect for me. Unfortunately, my son-in-law is allergic to cats. Can I leave Sasha with you?"

"I'll ask Mom," Anna said. "I'd love to take care of Sasha, but only if you promise to come back."

On the way home from the hospital, Anna was deep in thought while Mom sang along with the radio. Suddenly Anna asked, "Mom, why do think Dad took off?"

"I don't know, Anna. I've been puzzling over that, too. All we can be sure of is that there was some problem in him, not in us. Do you understand what I'm saying? We can feel hurt and angry, but we can't doubt ourselves. It's his loss."

"I was thinking that, too, Mom. Maybe someday Dad will come back and explain the mystery, but I'm not sure if I'll really care by then. Right now, I'm just glad I was there for Mrs. K. when she needed me."

"I'm there for you, too, baby. I won't let you down."

"I know, Mom, and we'll both be there for Billy."

Mom turned the radio up. She and Anna both sang along as they headed home.

The Clever Daughter

AN ORIGINAL STORY BY MARTHA JOHNSON

The pounding on the courtyard gate came just as Chang Liu's father finished her daily writing lesson. He put the brush down, careful not to spoil the perfect characters on the page, and nodded to Liu.

The gate shook from the fierce pounding. Liu had to fight the urge to run and answer. Instead she folded her hands and walked sedately, as befitted the only child of the head of the village. She opened the gate.

"Master Chang!" The man brushed past Liu as if she wasn't there. "I have a message from the magistrate."

Liu's heart thumped anxiously. The new magistrate was a greedy man, demanding one unfair tax after another from their poor village. What did he want now?

"The magistrate requires one hundred baskets of grain from this village." The man slapped an order on the table. "He will come here tomorrow to collect it."

One hundred baskets of grain! Liu covered her mouth to keep from protesting. If the village lost that much grain, there'd be nothing left in the storehouse for winter. The villagers would starve!

Father knew that—Liu could see it in his eyes. He'd tell the man they couldn't obey the order. Instead, her father bowed. "It will be as the magistrate commands."

When the gate had closed behind their unwelcome visitor, Liu couldn't keep silent. "Father! How could you agree? Why didn't you argue?"

Master Chang frowned. "One does not argue with one higher than oneself. How many times have I told you? At the top is the emperor, followed by the governor, the magistrate, the head of each village, then the men of each village. That is the order of things."

And at the very bottom are the women and children, Liu thought rebelliously. "But, Father…"

"No arguments, Liu." Father rubbed his forehead. "You will go to the storehouse and prepare the baskets. Tomorrow the grain goes to the magistrate."

Liu's stomach knotted with disappointment. How could he just give in? They had to do something!

Her father turned away tiredly, so Liu bowed and left the courtyard. But she wasn't ready to go to the storehouse—not yet. She wandered into the kitchen, where the cook was working on the evening meal. Soon there would be no food left to prepare. Liu's stomach growled as if it knew a hungry time was coming.

Liu watched the cook wrap dough around a bit of meat, preparing it for the pot. As she watched, an idea popped into her head—a daring idea to save the village.

Liu ran toward the storehouse. If her father wouldn't do anything, she would.

By the next day, Liu's father had worried himself sick, so it was easy to talk him into staying in bed. Liu told him she could handle turning over the grain.

When the magistrate and his men arrived, Liu waited outside the storehouse. A group of villagers looked on, and she could hear their murmuring voices.

"Foolish, to let a mere girl deal with the magistrate. As foolish as teaching her to read and write. He'll cheat her, and we'll be left with nothing."

The magistrate stepped forward, and Liu bowed. Her heart pounded loudly. If this didn't work…

"My father is ill," she said. "He has asked me to present the grain." She gestured to the children who had spent hours helping her last night. They began carrying out baskets as the magistrate's clerk counted. Liu cleared her throat. "We beg you, sir, please leave a little grain. Our storehouse is nearly empty."

The magistrate frowned. "Your taxes are required —one hundred baskets." The clerk whispered in his ear, and the magistrate's eyes lit with greed. Liu knew what the clerk was saying: there were not one hundred baskets, but one hundred and ten. She held her breath, waiting for the magistrate to point out her mistake.

He didn't. Instead, he gestured for his men to begin loading. A greedy, satisfied smile crept across his face.

Liu pulled out the receipt she had prepared. "My father directed me to have this receipt signed."

The magistrate gestured for the clerk to bring his writing materials, then he affixed his name and title. In a few moments the wagons were creaking away down the dusty road.

Liu's legs wobbled with relief. The children hurried to pull out the grain that they had hidden away. Master Chang, leaning on the cook's arm, peered into the storehouse just as they finished.

"Daughter, why is the grain still here? I saw the magistrate's carts go by with our baskets."

Liu smiled. "Baskets, yes, Father. Grain, no. The baskets are filled with chaff, with a little grain on top. That way I saved enough to feed the village all winter."

Liu's father went pale with shock. "Foolish girl, what have you done? We were ordered to turn the grain over. We had no choice but to obey."

Liu's chest hurt at her father's disappointment. "But, Father, I couldn't let the children starve. Besides, I…"

"Enough, enough. I can't listen. When the magistrate discovers this trick, he'll send soldiers to arrest us. We'll be tried before the governor himself."

"Father, my plan will work," Liu protested, but he didn't want to hear. Leaning heavily on the cook, he tottered back toward his room, leaving Liu to listen as the villagers muttered about her.

"Foolish girl, to think she could outwit a man. Now we will all have to pay for her foolishness."

Early the next morning, just as her father predicted, the soldiers came. They hauled Liu and her father off to the city. The villagers trailed along to see what would happen.

When Liu and her father arrived at the city square, the sun was riding high in the sky. The governor sat under the shade of a silken parasol while the magistrate's men lined the baskets up in front of him.

Liu's father bowed to the ground, and Liu did the same. Trembling, she waited for someone to speak.

With an outraged snarl, the magistrate began. "These two have cheated me of my taxes. The baskets this wicked girl gave me were filled with chaff."

He gestured to a soldier, who tipped one of the baskets on its side. A little golden grain spilled out, followed by a pile of chaff. The crowd gasped, and the governor frowned. He turned to Liu's father.

"Well, Master Chang? You are the head of your village. What have you to say for yourself?"

"It was not my father," Liu said quickly. "He was ill, and I gave the magistrate our grain."

The governor frowned at her. "Well? What is your excuse, girl?"

Liu took a deep breath. If she did what she'd planned, she had a chance to save the village. But what would her father think, with his obedience to the proper order of things? Would he ever forgive her?

"Honored governor, may I inspect these baskets?"

He waved his hand, and Liu walked solemnly along the rows of baskets. Then she stopped before him.

"I fear there has been a mistake," she said carefully. "How could these baskets have come from our village? The magistrate had an order for only one hundred baskets from us, and here are one hundred and ten."

The magistrate started to speak, but the governor held up his hand for silence. The governor's clerk began to count the baskets. When he had finished, he nodded. "One hundred and ten."

The governor turned to the magistrate. "How do you explain this?"

"The girl is lying," the magistrate blustered. "She's lying, that's all. I collected these baskets from her village, all right—one hundred and ten of them."

Liu pulled the receipt from her sleeve. "One hundred," she said clearly. "Here is a receipt, signed by the magistrate himself, for one hundred baskets. I'm sure the magistrate would not lie."

"But, but…" The magistrate's stammering was silenced by a wave of the governor's hand.

Everyone waited while the governor examined the receipt and talked with his advisors. Then he turned to the crowd. Liu held her breath. What would he say?

The governor spoke. "Master Chang and his clever daughter are free to go." He turned to the magistrate. "You will give them a bar of silver for their trouble. You will then reside in prison until we can learn how many other villages you have cheated."

The villagers crowded around Liu, and the children hugged her. "How clever she is," the villagers said. "How lucky Master Chang is to have such a clever daughter."

Liu looked anxiously at her father. The villagers' fickle praise meant little to her, and it would mean nothing if her father was still angry with her.

Her father closed his eyes for a moment, thinking deeply. Then he spoke. "At the top is the emperor, followed by the governor, the magistrate, the head man of the village, then the men of the village. That is the proper order of things." Liu's heart sank.

"However," her father continued, "my daughter did not show disrespect for the magistrate. Instead, she allowed him to expose himself as a cheat. So perhaps we should find room for a clever daughter in the proper order of things."

Liu bowed respectfully to her father. But she couldn't hold back a smile.

Like Father, Like Daughter

ADAPTED FROM A YIDDISH FOLKTALE BY
JONATHAN MARMELZAT

Hebrew Word:

Shiva (pronounced "SHI-va"): a seven-day period of mourning
following the funeral of a close relative.

In the city of Kiev, Ukraine, lived a prosperous banker named Moses Mordechai. He was known far and wide as a man of great integrity who always kept his word.

As he grew older he realized that he had everything in life he wanted, except a child. So he was overjoyed when, in his later years, his wife gave birth to a healthy daughter, Naomi. Moses Mordechai delighted in teaching her as she grew.

"A person is worth nothing if his word has no value," he told Naomi many times. "Always say what you mean and mean what you say."

One day, when Moses Mordechai was very old and very sick, Naomi sat on the edge of his bed and gently stroked his hand.

"Is there anything I can do for you, Father?" she asked.

"My lovely daughter," he smiled. "You have already done so much. I don't have long to live. I want you to know what a joy you have been to me in my old age and how much I love you."

"I love you, too, Father." Naomi leaned over to hug him.

After a few moments he said, "Now, I must make my final arrangements. Listen carefully to what I tell you." Naomi sat up straight and gave him her full attention.

"Your greedy uncle, Jacob, will come soon to hear my last will and testament. According to the law of our people, my brother must manage my estate, even though I do not trust him. I want you to know that I wish you and your mother to receive most of my fortune. Jacob may have a little for his trouble. If there is any dispute, you will be my witness. But you must listen very carefully to every word I tell him. Do you understand?"

"I understand, Father." Naomi squeezed his hand. "I will write it all down for you." She took a small paper scroll from her father's bedside table.

"I am very tired now." His eyes started to close. "Just remember what I said." With that he dozed off.

A short while later Naomi's uncle arrived at the house and was shown to his brother's bedroom. Naomi was still sitting at the edge of the bed.

"Please leave us alone," Uncle Jacob said, waving his hand towards the doorway. "This is men's business."

"I will stay as my father's witness," Naomi offered.

"A witness?" Uncle Jacob frowned. "For a conversation between brothers?"

"Naomi, please wait in the hallway," her father said. "But keep the door open and listen carefully in case I need you to bring me some water."

Naomi walked out of the room and set a chair just outside the door. Then she sat down, placed the paper scroll on her lap, dipped a pen into an ink bottle, and waited.

"My brother," Uncle Jacob said, stepping closer to the bed. "I have come to hear your last will and testament. I am ready to carry out your wishes." Naomi listened and recorded carefully as her father gave details of all the accounts at the bank.

"In each case I expect you to conduct business to the letter of my word," he instructed his brother.

"I will do exactly as you say," Uncle Jacob agreed. "And what about your estate and personal fortune? Of course there are your wife and daughter. How would you like me to take care of them?"

Moses Mordechai looked his brother straight in the eye, took a deep breath, and spoke his final words. "Give them whatever you want," he said, "and then keep the rest."

Naomi felt a shiver go down her spine as the two men embraced to seal their agreement. She could not believe what she had heard. "Has Father lost his senses?" she wondered. Nonetheless, she wrote down her father's exact words. Then she hid the scroll in a fold of her dress.

Her uncle was grinning greedily as he left the room. When Jacob was out of sight, Naomi went to her father's bedside and found him fast asleep. He never woke up again.

Hundreds of people attended the funeral. For many days Naomi and her mother were surrounded by visitors paying their respects. Naomi tried to be cordial, but her father's final words distracted her. "Give them whatever you want and then keep the rest." She kept hearing her father's voice. For several days she pondered the words carefully. Suddenly, one day, they finally made sense to her.

After *shiva* passed, Uncle Jacob came over to the house.

"You must prepare to move now," he announced.

"What do you mean?" Naomi protested. "This is our home."

"It is my home now." Uncle Jacob looked around the house. "You may go wherever you can afford to live on the allowance I have allotted to you."

"But that is not what my father wanted." Naomi looked him in the eye. "I am sure he wanted us to have…"

Uncle Jacob cut her off. "Your father instructed me to decide what you shall and shall not have."

"That is not what he said!" Naomi insisted.

"You dare question my word, child?"

Naomi stood up straight and took her mother's hand. "It is my father's words that count."

"Your father is not here anymore." Uncle Jacob said smugly. "So if you wish to contest my decision, you can take it up with the Rabbi's council."

"I will see to it that my father's words are obeyed." Naomi put her arm around her mother. "We will see you in council with the Rabbi."

The next day Naomi visited the Rabbi.

"Your situation poses an interesting predicament," the Rabbi told her. "You claim to know what your father wanted, but your uncle sees it differently. Without a witness it is just your word against his. And according to the law, I must defer to the word of a man over that of a child."

"What if I have a witness?" Naomi asked.

"You didn't say anything about a witness." The Rabbi studied her. "Who is your witness?"

"I cannot tell you just now. But if I have a witness, will you hear my case in council?" Naomi watched the Rabbi stroke his beard. After a few moments he spoke.

"Keeping a witness's identity secret is highly unusual. However, you have awakened my curiosity. I will call a meeting of the council for one week from today." He leaned forward and looked her in the eyes. "But remember, this is not a game. You must be prepared with your witness at that time."

"Thank you, Rabbi," Naomi said as she bowed to him and turned to leave. "I will be prepared."

On the day of the meeting, the council room was packed. Gossip about the case had spread across Kiev.

People couldn't believe the venerable banker would leave his wife and daughter at the mercy of his greedy brother. And everyone wanted to know the identity of Naomi's witness.

"Council will come to order," the Rabbi began. "We are here to resolve the dispute over the estate of Moses Mordechai. Will the parties involved in this matter please step forward." Uncle Jacob stepped to the front of the room. Naomi and her mother stood beside him.

"Now, young lady," the Rabbi looked at Naomi, "please tell us the nature of your claim."

"My uncle Jacob," Naomi started slowly, "has denied my mother and me the fortune my father intended to leave us." As whispers shot through the crowd, Uncle Jacob protested.

"Nothing could be further from the truth!" he shouted.

"Quiet, please!" The Rabbi waited for everyone to settle down. "We will get to the bottom of this matter in an orderly fashion. Now, Jacob Mordechai," the Rabbi turned to face him, "tell us what your brother instructed you to do."

"My brother told me to divide his fortune however I want."

"That's not true," Naomi interrupted. "He has not done what my father said."

"Hold your tongue, young lady!" the Rabbi warned. "You'll have to wait your turn." Naomi clenched her teeth and squeezed her mother's hand.

"And how is it that you want to divide the estate?" the Rabbi asked.

"I want my brother's house and most of his money," Uncle Jacob said. "Of course, I have set aside a small allowance for the maintenance of his family."

Naomi held her breath as she waited for the Rabbi's reaction. After a long silence he spoke.

"Moses Mordechai was a man of his word," the Rabbi said. "If you swear that you have spoken his words, then by law I must decree in your favor."

Naomi clenched her fist as Uncle Jacob smiled.

"But first," the Rabbi continued, "let us hear what the child Naomi has to say." He turned to look Naomi in the eyes. "You have heard the words of your uncle, and yet you claim to know otherwise. Please tell us what you know."

Naomi looked over at Uncle Jacob and began speaking cautiously.

"Before my father died," she turned to the Rabbi, "he told me to listen carefully to every word he said."

"Your father was a very wise man whose word was as good as gold," the Rabbi acknowledged. "But what does this have to do with the dispute? And how could you know what your father said to Jacob?"

"When Uncle Jacob came to my father's bedroom, my father asked me to keep the door open and listen carefully in case he needed some water," Naomi explained. "I heard every word my father said. My uncle has not told you his exact words."

"With all due respect to the council," Uncle Jacob smirked, "everyone knows my niece and I disagree about what my brother said. There's only one way to resolve this dispute. Isn't it time we heard from this witness of hers?" Uncle Jacob surveyed the room to see who would step forward.

"Your uncle is right," the Rabbi agreed. "We need a witness to resolve this dispute. Please call your witness now."

Naomi noticed the smile on Uncle Jacob's face as she reached into her cloak.

"My witness is already here," she said, smiling at her uncle. "Uncle Jacob is my witness."

"Oh, this is ridiculous!" Uncle Jacob snorted. The room buzzed with comments from the spectators.

"Quiet!" the Rabbi said before turning toward Naomi. "I thought you said you had another witness."

"I said I had a witness," Naomi said firmly. "Please let me continue."

"This is highly unusual," the Rabbi said, stroking his beard. "But I will allow it. Proceed."

"Go ahead, Uncle." Naomi turned to Jacob. "Tell the council exactly what my father said."

"I don't remember his exact words," Uncle Jacob admitted. "But I know what he meant, and I have done exactly…"

"I have something here," Naomi interrupted as she pulled the scroll out and held it in the air, "that might help my uncle remember my father's exact words. When I was in the hallway, I wrote down everything my father said. Here it is!" She opened the scroll and held it high so everyone could see.

"She could have written anything!" Uncle Jacob blurted out.

"Let me see that." The Rabbi held out his hand. Naomi handed him the scroll and waited as he read it.

"These are not the words of a child," he announced. "Let us proceed." He handed the scroll back to Naomi. "Tell us what it says."

"I will let my uncle tell you." Naomi turned and held the scroll in front of his eyes. "Is this what my father said?"

Uncle Jacob tugged at his beard as he read the scroll. He squinted as he thought for a moment before answering.

"Yes, it's all there," he finally agreed. "And as it says here at the end, Moses told me to give you whatever I want and then keep the rest. That's exactly what I am doing!" He folded his arms to emphasize his point.

"So you agree that these are my father's exact words?"

"Yes, but that's what I've been saying all along."

Naomi held the scroll high and began to read each word aloud.

"Give THEM," she said, pointing to her mother and herself, "whatever YOU WANT." She pointed to her uncle. "And THEN keep the rest."

A wave of whispers and chatter moved across the council room as Moses Mordechai's final words were heard and understood. The Rabbi nodded his head and stroked his beard as he looked at Naomi approvingly. He waited for the room to fall silent before turning his gaze on Uncle Jacob.

"You have told us that you want your brother's house and most of his money," the Rabbi said. "You must give THEM whatever YOU WANT."

Uncle Jacob's face turned beet red. Naomi looked at him triumphantly before she turned to hug her mother. Noticing the Rabbi's gaze, Naomi turned to face him.

"You are a very smart young lady," he said, smiling at her. "You have learned much from your father. He would be very proud of you. And we have learned today that like your father's, your word is as good as gold. From this day forth you will be known as Naomi, a woman of her word."